Down By The Sea

and Other Tales of Dark Destiny

Michelle Mellon

Printed in the United States of America

Michelle Mellon

**A HellBound Books LLC
Publication**

www.hellboundbookspublishing.com

Acknowledgements

It's been a long road to get here. Four of these stories have been published before, nine are new, and I'm thrilled to have them together as one fearsome family. For that, I thank the following people:

My parents, Bob and Marlene, my sister, Angela, and my husband, Larry, for their unconditional love and support.

My best friends, Amanda, Anne, Beth, Liz, and Strother, for shaping me into a better person without changing the nerdy weirdo within.

My friend Sara, for reading an early draft and asking the questions that fleshed out "Does Your Mother Know?"

James Longmore and the fantastic staff of HellBound Books for their professionalism, their love of the dark fiction genre, and their belief I have something to contribute to it.

Cover Art Designed by Patrick McEvoy

www.megaflowgraphics.com.

Down By The Sea

and Other Tales of Dark Destiny

Michelle Mellon

CONTENTS

Michelle Mellon

Crawlspace

Old Lady Ennis must have called my mom after me and Slow Jimmy climbed the fence. Slow Jimmy is smaller than me so he pulled himself up and over real quick. When I finally scraped and huffed and puffed myself over, he was nowhere in sight. Not that we could have seen much anyway, what with the old lady's house being on the back corner lot with no streetlights around.

I hitched up my pants and hissed, "Jimmy! Where you at?"

I heard some shuffling near the back door.

"Jimmy! Is that you? This ain't funny, man!"

I started to move towards the noise but it stopped. I stopped.

Seconds later, the whole yard lit up. I covered my eyes and backed up till I hit the fence. Somehow I managed to grab a hold and fling myself over the top. Then I ran.

The next morning my mom was standing over me, hands on hips. "What time did you get home last night, AJ?"

"I dunno. Slow Jimmy had the watch and I lost him."

Shit. I sat up in bed and watched her eyes narrow and her lips scrunch up. Then she was off.

"How many times have I told you not to call that boy slow? Where's your watch? What were you two doing last night?"

She stopped, waiting for me to confess--to "own" my actions like it said in that parenting book she brought home a couple of months ago. I figured she'd already talked to Old Bag Ennis, so if she already knew what I was doing, she should talk to me about it straight up.

"Nothing." I shrugged. "We were just hanging out, ya know? Sl-uh, Jimmy wandered off and I figured I should head home." I held my breath. All she did was shake her head. The beginning of her *I'm so disappointed in you* trip again.

"What am I gonna do with you, AJ?" she'd always ask.

"I don't know," I'd always say with my head hung low.

Then she might blame herself, but usually she'd blame my dad for not being a good role model. Today, though, her head stopped shaking and she stared at me. Hard. Then she caught me off guard, swooping in and grabbing me by my T-shirt.

"I've had enough of your selfishness and arrogance. I won't be embarrassed one more time by the cops bringing you home, AJ. Next it'll be that knock in the middle of the night, asking me to come identify my sixteen-year-old son at the morgue. I don't know what's wrong with you. Do you even care?"

Her face was inches from mine; I could see her nostrils marching in and out, see the smooth skin of her upper lip that she covered in goop every other Saturday afternoon, smell her spearmint toothpaste. She had one of my dreads trapped under her thumb. When she shook me it tugged at my head, but I wouldn't look in her eyes. No way.

"Get dressed," she said, shoving me back down onto the bed and looking at the poster on the wall instead of at me. "After breakfast you're going over to Mrs. Ennis's house to help her with some projects she's got going."

"Uh uh! I ain't going over to Old Lady—"

Her eyes sliced down to me so fast I thought I could hear my poster rip in half. I had never seen my mother look so angry, not even that afternoon a few years ago when I got home from school and she was in the hallway, shaking, balling up the note my dad left before taking off with some chick from his office.

I scooted across the bed away from her to the dresser, where I stood up and made a show of rifling through the drawers till I knew she was gone.

I walked the four blocks to the old lady's house in the street (no sidewalks in our neighborhood, just the way all the old folks liked it). She was sitting in a rusty, creaky metal glider on the front porch, wearing one of those ugly dresses with pink and blue and yellow flowers like my great-grandmother would wear. Instead of letting the glider swing freely, she kept her thick-soled white shoes firmly planted on the painted wood porch, and sorta rocked forward and back.

I trudged up the short path from the street to the steps of the porch and waited. Eventually she screwed up her face and squinted up at me.

"Oh, it's you," she said in her shaky voice that always reminded me of a rock tumbler I had as a kid. "Well come on up here and sit with me, Anthony." She never called me "AJ" like everybody else.

She patted the seat next to her on the glider. I sat on the fraying white wicker chair across from her instead.

That squinting sure didn't help all those wrinkles. She looked like someone stuck a cotton-covered walnut on top of a little tiny body. Her hands were bony but the skin was pretty smooth, and her legs somehow didn't have that saggy look old ladies' legs get 'cause their stockings keep drooping down.

"My mom said you had some stuff you needed help with." The last thing I wanted to do was sit around on a Saturday afternoon and chat with some old lady.

"I been in this house for 55 years, Anthony. You know that?"

"Yeah."

"In my day, we answered our elders with respect. Seems like none of you are mindful of your manners these days."

I just looked down at the scuffmarks on the toes of my sneakers from climbing her fence the night before.

"All you boys out here at all hours doing Lord-knows-what. Getting shot and acting like it's no big deal. Running around with hussies who feel no shame in having babies and losing track of which daddy each baby has. All of you looking for just enough space to crawl around in, none of you willing to stand up and be men."

I heard the sigh before I realized it came from my mouth. I looked up and sure enough, nothing was wrong with the old lady's ears. She pursed her lips and squinted her eyes at me, shaking her head. I half-expected her to ask, *What am I gonna do with you, Anthony?* Instead, she pushed herself out of the glider and stood in front of me.

"First you're going to mow my lawn. You be sure to dig up those dandelions first. You hear me?"

"Uh huh."

"The yard tools are in the shed out back. When you're done, put them back where you found 'em and knock on the back door."

I tugged open the rusty sliding door of the shed and found a digging tool and a push mower I dragged around to the front yard. Old Lady Ennis hadn't moved from her spot on the porch.

"Don't forget to weed first. Nasty things are always spreading around and setting up roots too quickly where they're not wanted."

I scanned the grass on one side of the walk and stooped down to dig out a dandelion plant. Behind me I heard the screen door bang shut as she went into the house. I knew she was still watching, though, so I kept wandering around, digging up dandelions and dumping them in a pile on the walkway. When I was done weeding and mowing I put the tools away but tossed the dead weeds in her vegetable garden.

I knocked on the back door and she opened it enough to hand me a glass.

"Here's some lemonade, Anthony. Drink that up while you dust yourself off, then I need you to come in and help me move some boxes."

Inside, the house was all furniture polish waxed and museum perfect. I mean, my mom liked the house to be neat, but it was like nobody actually lived in Old Lady Ennis's house. And the whole place was filled with the kind of crap my mom always drooled over when we passed antique stores.

She stopped at the top of the stairs. "You see that room there?" She pointed down the hall. "I need you to move the boxes stacked up in there into the closet in this spare bedroom here," she said, indicating the room in front of us.

"What's in the boxes?"

She stared at me. I shrugged and moved down the hall. The boxes were under the window against the far wall. Something shiny caught my eye as I moved toward them. On top of a dresser, in front of some ancient pictures in silver frames, was a switchblade. The real tough kind, like you see in old movies.

"Now that you're done gawking, you can get to movin' those boxes."

Damn! Even in those clunky shoes she had managed to sneak up behind me without making a sound. I sighed and started hauling. By the fifth trip, my back hurt and my fingers were sore. By the tenth trip I was out of patience, energy, and, thankfully, almost out of boxes. I stared longingly at the knife. I saw myself opening up some of those tightly taped boxes with it; see what kind of treasure lay inside. I also thought of some pretty inventive ways to use the knife on the old lady.

"That pocketknife belonged to my Eugene, bless his soul."

I jumped. She had done it again, and I knocked over one of the picture frames in my surprise.

"I gave it to him on our wedding day," she said, reaching past me to set the frame back up. "See? That's us there." She pointed to the picture, still in her hand. "Still works, even these ten years or so since he's been gone, and I don't even oil it like he used to."

Now I *knew* she was batty. First off, the couple in that picture was from, like, a hundred years ago. Second, my mom moved into the neighborhood when she was a little girl, and she said Old Mr. Ennis had been dead long before then.

"No, they don't make things like that any more," she babbled on. "Too worried about doing things the fast and easy way to make money. Nobody willing to put in the work any more." She sorta clucked her tongue and wandered into the hallway.

Surely I deserved some reward for putting up with this – something other than endless glasses of sugary lemonade. I turned and grabbed the last (and largest) box. I staggered a little and sat the box on the dresser, panting for show in case she popped back in the room unexpectedly. I slipped the knife into my fingers under the box and made the last trip into the spare bedroom.

"You done all right, Anthony," she said, surveying the room.

I hadn't bothered to stack the boxes neatly after the first couple of trips, so I knew she was either senile or eager to get me out of the house.

"Come on down with me to the kitchen and I'll get you another glass of lemonade."

I gritted my teeth. With shaking hands, I fingered the knife, now in my pocket. I could probably make a lot of money selling her stuff. Quit school and make it out on my own. But how could I get her out of the way and make it look like an accident?

That's when I remembered the crawlspace. Old Lady Ennis was one of the few people on our street who hadn't converted hers to a basement. Slow Jimmy and I looked in his crawlspace once. Nobody'd go in if they didn't have to, but it was a good place to hide things. If I could just get her to call my mom to tell her I was done and coming home…

"Have a seat at the table, Anthony."

I pulled out one of the black metal chairs and the feet scooted stubbornly across the linoleum. The kitchen smelled of lemonade and lemon dishwashing soap and lemon floor wax. All shriveled up and sour, like the old lady. I smiled to myself.

"I got just one more thing for you to do, Anthony." She handed me a glass and walked over to the back door to look out into the yard. "Real easy, this one, but the most important."

"No way!" I slammed the glass down on the table, spilling lemonade over the sides. "I'm done, and I'm going home. You can't force me to stay here and do no more of this crap."

"So that's it?" She clomped on over to me and stuck one of those bony fingers in my face. "Just a few hours of work and you're ready to quit? How many days of work you think it took to buy you them clothes, or the food you eat, or that house you live in? You ever think of that?"

I stood up, pushed past her, and stalked out the back door.

"Anthony, I'm not done with you!" she cried before the back door slammed shut behind me.

I turned the corner and headed for the front of the house.

"The least you're gonna do is give me back my Eugene's knife."

I stopped in my tracks. Not because she found out I had the knife, but because her voice was soft and close enough to raise the hairs on the back of my head. I turned around.

She was right behind me.

"I had high hopes for you, Anthony. Thought you might be different than the other boys."

She circled around me so she stood between me and the path to the gate at the front of the house. I smiled. She weighed what – ninety pounds? But she was still talking and pointing and I backed up just to get away from that finger in my face.

"Thought you might be willing to work hard, show you got it in you. Looks like you failed."

I tripped and fell backwards over a large, dusty bag.

"Now you open that bag and you spread some of that quicklime in under my crawlspace. Got a rat problem, just like them weeds. Except they have the nerve to go and die and leave their contaminating smell up under my house."

I stood and brushed myself off.

"I told you, I'm done. You want the smell gone, you take care of it yourself."

I flicked the knife open in my pocket. The crawlspace entrance was right there. Only problem was, my mom would probably call and check in with the old lady after I got home. I could force Old Lady Ennis to call my mom, and then get rid of her. Maybe I wouldn't have to use the knife, or maybe just enough to scare her into a heart attack or something. Or I could just go in the house, grab some stuff, and take off for good.

"I always do, Anthony, I always do."

"Wha–?" I looked back at the old lady, trying to figure out what she was talking about. Except she wasn't looking so old any more. With her back unbent she could almost meet me eye-to-eye. I was so caught up in watching the wrinkles disappear from her gnarled face that, too late, I saw her fleshy hands shoot out and grab a shovel propped up near the bag of quicklime.

There was a flash of metal. I struck out blindly with the knife, but didn't connect.

She did.

I heard my jaw and teeth crack. I tasted blood. I smelled the damp earth as I fell down into it.

* * *

"He didn't come home, Mrs. Ennis. When did AJ leave here?"

"Didn't finish the work I needed him to do," the old woman muttered. "Marched off."

"I can't believe that boy!"

"All he's done is cause you grief, child. It's time for you to let go."

Footsteps. Then, "How about a glass of lemonade? It's always worked to cheer up the other mothers when their children go astray."

"I don't know what we'd do without you. You've been such a rock for all of us. How do you do it?"

"Makes me mad to see how things have gotten. If you're gonna fight it, though, you gotta draw strength from it, feed off it. Yup, been enough bad in this world to keep me going a long time now," she chuckled.

* * *

The air down here is stale. Sometimes there's a breeze, puffing up swirls of dust and gritty drops of rat shit that land on my face and lips. Spiders crawl up my legs, looking for shelter and warmth in my groin. The piles stuffed into the corners sometimes spill in a clacking pool around me. I thought I caught a glimpse of Slow Jimmy before the latest wave of yellowed, fang-scarred bones blocked my view.

You'd think the worst part would be the smell, but Old Lady Ennis was smart about all that quicklime. Even with all of the others down in here with me--the other guys from the neighborhood who just seemed to disappear and nobody seemed to miss them too much--even with all that decay, I cling mostly to the savory scent of my own self.

I wanna scream, but my throat's raw from swallowing bits of broken teeth. My jaw grates anyway when I try to move it, and I bit off most of my tongue with the old lady's first blow with the shovel. I'm waiting for the pain to pass. It's not nearly as bad as the cold, though.

It's so cold.

"Won't be needing them clothes any more." I hear her voice echo in my head, over and over; followed by the tearing of fabric in a last, long flash of that knife I wanted so badly.

"Got a nice box ready for your things." She grins. "Just like all the others."

Crash Test Dummy

Bradley Denton sat on his favorite stool at the Corner Six Bar and Grill in Keyes, Oklahoma, and raised his beer mug in tribute to himself.

"I beat it!" he cried.

Pete the bartender glanced up from the glassware he was wiping. He nodded at Bradley, the frown just perceptible above his greying eyebrows, then looked back down and focused on his task.

Bradley swiveled around on the padded barstool like a child, raising his glass in turn to the older couple in the booth behind him and the only other patron, a woman sitting at the far end of the bar. The older couple looked up, smiled, and went back to their meal. The woman continued sipping her drink without looking at Bradley.

He put down his glass and repeated his spin on the stool, this time losing his balance and slapping his hands down on the bar to catch himself. They made a satisfying *thunk* on the scarred wood, and he slapped them down again, as if emphasizing his point.

Pete put down his towel, sighed, and walked over to where Bradley sat.

"Anything else for you, Bradley, or can I ring up your tab?"

"Peter my good man." Bradley took a large swallow from his mug. "I'll have another." He tilted the glass back until the last of the beer and foam slid into his mouth, then set the mug down heavily and smiled.

"Do you think that's a good idea? I mean, after today shouldn't you try to take it easy for a while?"

"I don't pay you to think," Bradley snipped. "I pay you to pour."

Pete glanced at the other patrons. The couple began whispering and looked at Bradley as they hurriedly paid their bill and left. The woman at the end of the bar continued to sip her drink, seemingly unaware of her surroundings. Pete leaned over and spoke softly.

"The thing is, Bradley, you're drawing too much attention to yourself around here. The boss, well, he's a little nervous. If something else happened, people might start to thinking to hold us responsible."

Bradley slapped his hands down on the bar again and smiled at the sound. Pete winced and leaned back, his hands scrabbling under the counter until he felt the comforting solidity of the bat always strapped within reach. Pete had never liked Bradley Denton. Bradley was loud and boorish, wealthy enough to feel entitled, and cold-hearted in the bargain. He had amassed a small army of lawyers to beat this latest DUI charge. Somehow he escaped with only a community service sentence and a small fine for the girl who was permanently injured by his reckless driving. As satisfying as it might have been to him personally, Pete still hoped he wouldn't have to use the bat.

"So that's how it is, is it?" Bradley looked down the bar to see if the woman was paying attention. She and the waitress were negotiating an item on the menu, oblivious to Bradley and Pete's discussion.

"I've been coming here every day for three years. This is my seat," Bradley said, slipping off the stool again and stumbling before securing his hold on its thick edge.

"It's been four years, Bradley, and that ain't the issue. Three months ago you left here and you drove home and 'bout killed a little girl riding her bike."

"But I didn't. And I know better now. I've changed."

"I wish I could believe that. Al wishes he could believe that. But you're a liability to us, Bradley. You're gonna have to tone it down until things cool off a bit."

Bradley shoved himself away from his bar stool, jabbing his finger in the air at Pete as he left.

"Put it on my tab."

He bumped around in the wood-paneled entryway a bit before he got a grasp on the front doors and pulled himself out into the night. The temperature had dropped considerably. Bradley had a coat in his car but wasn't yet ready to admit defeat. He dug in his pockets for a cigarette and lighter and stomped around the gravel parking lot of the Corner Six, cigarette dangling from his teeth, slapping his arms to stay warm.

With false bravado Bradley thought of how he'd wait around to jump Pete after his shift, and show him how hot things could really get. Or maybe he'd take his cigarette and use it to spark a little heat for Al and his precious bar and reputation. He smiled a bit at the thought. Then he practiced the derisive curl he'd use during his imaginary pummeling of Pete or his incendiary salute to the bar itself.

But it was cold and Bradley got bored easily. So he crushed out the cigarette and tried to remember where he'd parked his car. The truth was, the Corner Six was the last refuge he had. He was a social drinker; he didn't like going to the liquor store and bringing stuff home to drink alone (although he had a stash in the cabinet for those really hard mornings or evenings).

He didn't even live in Oklahoma. But with so many problems from before, he was willing to cross the state line regularly for a drink. And there'd been no trouble until that girl on her bike, zooming out in front of him from nowhere and getting herself caught up in the grill of his truck. Sooner or later his lawyers wouldn't be able to keep his punishment to mere fines and community service. Still, he reflected, almost proudly, three DUIs and four DWIs and he was going strong.

It was the getting home that was the hard part. His wife repeatedly suggested he pay for a driver. Then she left him after the incident with the girl. It was true, he had the money for a driver, but he preferred his independence. And he liked his monstrous SUV. And he wanted to save his money for the bar. And, he grinned, thinking of the paltry amount of alimony his soon-to-be-ex-wife was asking for, now he could use that money on other women.

Bradley was still grinning when he climbed up into his silver land yacht and brought the engine to life. He imagined himself as part of that beer commercial with the big silver bullet that zoomed around, bringing the party to the people. He stomped on the gas and gravel spun out from under his tires, leaving dings on the three other cars in the lot. His car lurched forward and up onto the blacktop, and Bradley began the drive home.

It was several miles before he realized he was heading south, toward Texas, instead of west. The road was deserted on a late Wednesday evening, so Bradley pulled across the median and got back on in the direction of the Corner Six. He had left the bar in such a huff and hurry he'd forgotten to use the restroom before hitting the road. The pressure in his bladder increased, along with his annoyance at having missed his turn. There was no way around it; he'd have to pull over and relieve himself.

The scenery stretched out before him for miles. Bradley scanned the horizon for a likely spot before realizing there was no one else out on the road, so any place would be as good as any other. He drove onto the shoulder, hopped out without looking around, and scurried around the front of the car. Even though he was alone, he thought, he didn't need any trouble if somebody happened along. He moved off the road until he was out of the glow cast by the headlights, then unzipped his pants and sighed with relief as the pressure eased.

It took Bradley a moment to figure out where the roar was coming from--it was familiar, but out of context. He turned and watched as a figure sitting in his car gunned the engine and drove away.

That was it. Now he was royally screwed. He was standing in a gully off the side of the road in the dark in the middle of nowhere, with no phone and urine bouncing off the tips of his leather shoes.

He began an awkward dance – zipping up his pants and shaking his shoes while trying to get back to the road to see where his car was headed. He looked both ways. Just like when he first pulled off the road, there was no one around. If possible, it seemed even darker and emptier out there than before.

Bradley turned his head once again. Headlights flashed on and he stood, transfixed, as a car materialized out of the darkness and rolled slowly toward him. It was *his* car, he realized. He stepped out into the road and started forward to meet it.

It stopped a few feet away. Bradley stopped, too. The car's interior light came on and Bradley could see a woman behind the wheel. There was something, something in her face that he needed to know. Something important, he felt. But he couldn't focus and was a little confused about what was happening, and realized he had grown really cold out there on the side of the road.

The interior light switched off.

Bradley tried again to remember what it was he knew about the woman.

Now the headlights switched off.

The Corner Six. He had seen her there. There, and someplace else. He was still trying to figure out the someplace else when the headlights flashed on and somehow that roaring behemoth of his had snuck up within arm's length of where he stood.

Bradley shielded his eyes and his car moved quickly into reverse. It hovered, waiting, growling, just long enough for him to remember with a sudden pang of fear where he had seen the woman before. Then the car shot forward, making contact. There was a deep thud, and Bradley was catapulted sideways into the shadows of the shoulder.

The first thing that terrified him was the fact that he woke up. And he felt nothing. He was laying in a ditch in the middle of nowhere and no one knew where he was and, if he were being honest with himself for the first time in a really long time, no one would really care anyway.

The second thing that terrified him was that he was wrong on one point. One person knew where he was. She was standing over him with a flashlight. He could see the light move closer and then farther away. She was probably checking out how badly she had broken him.

Bradley felt a small spark of hope. Maybe this was a misunderstanding. A prank taken too far and she felt sorry and was going to get him some help. Then she turned the flashlight on herself and leaned over so he could see and hear her as she spoke to him.

"How does it feel?"

And there it was, the third and final thing that terrified Bradley Denton. Beyond recognizing her face from the Corner Six, he finally remembered where else he had seen this woman. A face he had actively avoided in the courtroom. But those deep, dark eyes could not be mistaken. They were the same. The same as that little girl when she turned them wide upon him before he plowed her down. She had her mother's eyes.

"Can you even feel anything any more?" she asked. "Do you have a conscience? A soul? Or do all those dollars you spend to clean up your messes make *everything* go away?"

Bradley's fear turned to outrage. Oh, she had no idea. No one spoke to him or treated him this way and got away with it. He was going to use "all those dollars" to make this bitch pay. If it took everything he had, he'd own her.

The woman was speaking again, looking at Bradley but not really seeing him. The words sounded sing-songey, like a chant or a prayer. Some kind of New Age or Indian bullshit. Bradley still had the presence of mind to scoff, before his remaining senses started to dull and he closed his eyes.

One way or another, this would all be over soon. He would be rescued and she'd pay for what she'd done, or he'd be dead and sleeping peacefully forever with the troubles of this world far behind him. Revenge or rest, he would be happy either way.

But when Bradley opened his eyes again, he realized they were the only things he could move. He couldn't speak. His jaw wouldn't even open. He couldn't turn his head. It was bright and loud. He smelled rubber, paint, and other strong chemicals. In his line of sight was the dashboard of a car, with his hands propped stiffly on the steering wheel. But he couldn't feel it beneath his fingers. He couldn't feel his body on the seat. Or his feet, floating below him he presumed, on the pedals.

From somewhere outside the vehicle he heard, "Front impact crash test, car number nine-two-seven, in three, two, one."

The car sped forward, straight into a barrier, and the one thing Bradley *did* feel was his world shift to slow motion. The front of the car rippled back toward him. The windshield cracked and shattered as the frame bent, spraying glass across the dashboard. Bradley's body jerked forward and caught in the seatbelt as the air bag deployed, slamming him back into the seat. His hands flew off the steering wheel, a couple of fingers bent at awkward angles. Now Bradley felt a dull pain across his chest and a sharp pain in his face and neck. After an eternity the car rolled backward. Bradley waited for someone to check on him, but no one approached the car.

He wanted to scream or bang his intact fingers on the steering wheel or beat his head against the window. He wanted to make someone hear him, see him, sympathize with his plight. It wasn't fair. Why was this happening to him?

Things were black for a while. Then came the bright lights and loud sounds and the mechanical smells. From somewhere outside the vehicle Bradley heard the same emotionless voice.

"Side impact crash test, car number five-one-three, in three, two, one."

Bradley closed his eyes, hoping it was all some horrible nightmare. The car sped forward and then was hit on the driver's side, where Bradley was sitting. His left shoulder popped and his elbow flattened a bit. Something sharp pierced his side and his hip felt out of place. Bradley took comfort in the fact that after an initial spike, the pain seemed to even out, lessening, leaving him numb again.

He hoped this was it; he was finally dying and at worst he would be a bodiless consciousness floating in space. But things just went black, and when he woke up it was to the same bright light and big noise and bad scent as before.

"Rear impact crash test, car number seven-five-eight, in three, two, one."

Bradley felt numb on the edges but a burning awakening at his core. He was angry. He knew the girl's mother was somehow responsible for this. Sure, he had made his mistakes, but he fixed them all. Did she want more money? He could take care of that easily, just like he had taken care of all of the broken cars and broken people in his past.

Except he had no way to tell anybody.

The car was slammed from behind and Bradley's face thumped against the steering wheel and snapped back against the unforgiving headrest. In a couple of his past accidents the other drivers and their quack doctors talked about head injuries. Something about the brain rattling around in the skull. Bradley had sneered; clearly people were constructed more strongly than that. But now he felt it for himself--the sensation that someone had thrown a ripe melon into a small bucket and kicked it down the stairs.

How was it possible to feel so much pain and still be so numb, he wondered?

* * *

"Front impact crash test, car number four-two-nine, in three, two, one."

Bradley's eyes were open. They were always open now. He was still paralyzed. He couldn't speak. In his line of sight he could see the dashboard of the car, with his hands propped stiffly on the steering wheel. Somewhere below he knew hung the rest of his body, but it didn't matter. He never felt anything until the point of impact. Then every ligament, tendon and muscle in his body strummed to life like a crash-test chorus.

He knew he was being punished. Bradley thought that perhaps, if he could feel something besides anger and a sense of injustice, it might be the key to his release. But he couldn't. It wasn't in him. He had no guilt, no shame, no empathy, no remorse. It wasn't even in him to feel sadness or disappointment at that revelation.

With something akin to a resigned sigh, Bradley accepted the truth. It was clear now that all of those people were right. The families and the lawyers and the judges and the people who looked askance at him in the bar, outside the courtroom, on the street. There was no hope in him, no light, no life, no humanity. He was, and always had been, a walking shell. The glare and the loud and the brief moments of feeling were his reality now-- his brief, periodic escapes from being permanently numb.

Somebody's Angel

Measure twice, cut once. That's what papa and mama always used to say. There used to be a time I listened to every word that passed through their lips. I thought they knew the why and the how of all of life and could do no wrong. I did my chores and my homework without complaint and even stopped going to school when they said I'd had enough learning from strangers. I would have given anything for them to tell me how proud they were of me.

But that never happened.

Still, Papa at least tried to hide his disappointment that I wasn't a boy. That's why I'd stand out there with him in that workshop of his in the garage and learn about awls and saws and woodworking craft. He took me camping and fishing and hunting and taught me how to dress a carcass and tan a hide.

Then I'd go inside with mama and learn about sewing pretty dresses and perfect curtains. I practiced cleaning the unders and insides of things as well as the on-tops and arounds, and making lip-licking stew from the meat

I'd hunted or melt-in-your-mouth buttery cakes. Between the two of them, there wasn't much time for me to make many friends my own age, and live a teenage life like I saw in all those magazines down at the newsstand in town.

I didn't mind at first, trying to please them both and leaving nothing in the way of joy for myself. They brought me into this world--as they liked to remind me-- so I owed them as much. And I'd have to take care of them when they were older and helpless, so I'd need some skills to land a job (said papa) or a man (said mama).

After a while, though, I watched the people I once went to school with - and then their younger brothers and sisters, go off to start exciting new lives away from this place. I began to wonder if I would be stuck here forever, living in this 9x9 room papa added on when mama got pregnant after they'd been trying for near-twenty years and finally given up. Would I spend an eternity watching the sun come up through the knot holes in the wood, feeling the wind through the gaps in the planks, and sleeping on hand-me-down sheets so old and worn I was afraid to turn in my sleep or I'd shred them like tissue paper?

I'm a hateful and ignorant girl, I know. Not to mention disrespectful and unappreciative. Papa pulled those last two words out of the air one day like a magician had hid a dictionary up in the smoke curling out of his pipe. He wasn't one for a lot of speaking, and certainly not with words long enough to wrap down to another line in a book. And mama just stood there nodding her head like there was nothing out of the ordinary about it and she heard talk like that every day. Even from him.

Useless sheep. Stupid bitch.

They told me about using that kind of language. I still have burns from the fresh-made lye soap mama used to wash out my mouth the last time I spoke a cuss word. Since then I'd just been practicing them in my head. Each time I heard a new word (mostly from the guys at the construction site I walked past on my way to the store), I'd roll it around silently on my tongue. I'd exaggerate the shape to feel my teeth and my lips move around each dirty, God-slapping syllable.

And it felt good. Real good, like there couldn't possibly be any bad mixed up in it. Good like the first time one of those guys from the construction site wrapped his lips around mine--around those same lips and teeth that'd been practicing those sinful words. That was a double-good feeling right there.

Papa and mama knew they were making me a different kind of life and they didn't care. They said they had done what they did to try to keep me away from a world that was so far gone from the right and the moral and the just, that it ate up misguided girls like me and doomed them forever to a life of sin and an afterlife of eternal suffering. So they pulled me out of school to keep me free of evil influences and kept me busy with things not likely to lead me to the devil's lair.

Guess I found my way there anyway. In fact, I'd followed the bread crumbs or the yellow brick road or the red carpet right up into Satan's shack of sin, 'cause I'd gone behind their backs and kissed that boy from the construction site and then kissed another and then given my whole self up to a third.

They said what happened to me was a blessing as well as a vengeance. That I should know that even when they weren't able to watch me, I was being watched, and my sins were being recorded for a future reckoning. I told them if they had gone ahead and signed my permission slip for those sexual education classes while

I was still in school, then maybe I wouldn't have tried to see what I was missing.

Of course I only sassed them like that because by then it was too late and I knew I wouldn't get a whipping for it. They wanted to throw me out, I know they did, but they wanted to punish me more. I think they were jealous that it took them so long to have me, and here I was, on my first time, carrying a baby inside. Plus, they were getting along in years and all. I mean, mama had me when she was forty-five and here I was almost seventeen and already my own woman, and they knew I'd be the only one around to take care of them. Looked like we were all stuck with each other, sin or not.

I figured this might be my last chance to mean something to someone, anyhow. No one got all soft-like when they saw me, or smiled and said how much they missed me when I wasn't around or how empty their life would be without me. No one needed me yet. Seemed like all those years of trying left no joy for mama and papa when I finally did arrive, and that boy that started a life growing in me barely got around to calling me by my name, let alone calling me his "darling" or "precious one" or "angel."

The spring grew into summer, which dragged into fall. My whole life had become one long chore, all the while carrying another person around inside of me. I was tired and out of sorts and mama and papa spared no chance to tell me how I had brought it upon myself. I was moody and it didn't help that once I started to get really fat they wouldn't let me leave the house any more so I wouldn't shame them in front of the neighbors.

Thanksgiving was a hollow day. Papa did it up right like he did every year with the blessing, but he didn't make any mention of the baby. It's not like it weren't obvious that there was really four of us at the table now. I mean, I had to scoot my chair back and pretty much balance my plate on top of baby-to-be's head to be able to get at my food. And mama outdid herself with the desserts, but wouldn't let me have nothing more than ice cream on account of how she said all the rest of it would just make me fat and wouldn't add nothing to what was good for the baby.

They flip-flopped like that all the time; one of them mentioning the baby at every chance to point out why what I did was wrong or hurtful, and the other pretending I was just in a chunky phase and there wasn't going to be a squalling ball of life waiting at the end of it all.

Whichever of them was in a baby-friendly mood would work on their Christmas gift for the baby. That's the way we did it in our house, each of us making a gift for the others instead of spending money on store-bought stuff that wouldn't hold up as long or be as practical as what we could do with our own hands. I guess since this year there was going to be me and the baby to provide for, they decided to work together on the baby's gift.

I figured me and the baby were already nearly done working together on a gift for them. *The baby*. Turns out thinking a thought like that and saying it out loud were two different sides of the same idea.

One early morning Mama was in the kitchen making up a batch of brownies from scratch. It wasn't any special occasion so she must have been mad at me for something and was doing it out of spite. She knew they were my favorite. (Well, maybe they were a tie with her special peanut butter cookies.)

I knew how it would go. She'd pull those brownies out of the oven with the crunchy crust and the warm soft insides that still dripped a little bit of chocolate, and she and Papa would sit at the table with their treat and their cold glasses of milk and I would only be allowed milk on account of the baby.

Papa was out in his workshop, probably finishing up the baby's gift, staying out of mama's pettiness like he always did. Feeling hungry and angry and wanting to be just as mean as mama, I went to the back of the house to my sad little add-on room. I dug under the mattress and came up with my prize: a book.

Mama and papa never kept any books in the house. When they pulled me out of school I hadn't told them I had a library card. For those first few months I'd get a few books to read whenever I went on my weekly trips to the store. When they stopped letting me go to the store I still had books out on loan, and I lied when the overdue notices showed up in the mail, saying it must have been some kind of mistake. I'd read those books so many times over by now that I almost knew them by heart, but I waddled back up to the front with one cradled in my arm, library sticker on the outside plain as day.

Mama was putting the brownies in the oven. I waited, but she stood up with her back toward me and moved sideways to the sink to begin washing the dishes.

"I'm going outside to read a spell," I said, waiting for her head to whip around so I could wiggle that book in her face.

"Do whatever you want," she sighed, still not turning to look at me and give me my due.

I waited a couple more minutes but she kept scrubbing away at her mixing bowl and measuring things, so I huffed my way through the front door and plopped down on the porch steps. The book didn't hold any charm any more, so I pushed it off to the side. I leaned back, enjoying the smell of baking chocolate through the screen and the breeze that had just started turning cool in these few days before Christmas. It made me a little sad. No snow likely this year.

With the last of the dishes drying and the brownies safely in the oven, I guess mama decided it was finally time to set her sights on me. I felt her standing at the screen door, watching me. After a while she asked why she hadn't seen me working on a gift for the baby. Come to think of it, she said, she hadn't seen me working on much of anything these days.

I didn't even turn around. I should have been mad, what with her calling me lazy and fat and shameful all the time like she did, but I was calm. I was so calm I surprised myself with it. I told her I didn't have anything to give my baby but the rest of the space in my tiny room out back, which wasn't much bigger than the space it was laying in right then. Then I told her what I'd been thinking--that my gift to her and papa was due to arrive any day now, and wouldn't they be happy with their one-of-a-kind, fresh-made granbaby?

That got her hollering and stamping around looking for something to take it out on. Whatever she ripped, threw, tore, or spilled I was gonna get blamed for and then told to put to rights. So I pushed myself up off the porch and headed out to the workshop with papa to see what he was working on.

I guess he knew I was coming because he already had a sheet over the gift by the time I got inside. He turned to me and wanted to know what all the noise was about. I told him the same thing I told mama. He stood there for a second, the red rising up over his collar and into his face. And his hands started to tremble, like they were the source of all that blood rushing to his head and couldn't operate right without it.

I hadn't seen him this mad since he first found out about the baby, but I just didn't care any more. Mama was out on the porch now yelling about the library book and what a truly sinful and deceitful girl I was, then she started crying and I heard the screen door slam.

That's when it happened.

Papa raised his arm to me, fist crowning the end of it, ready to purge all his anger over the baby and the books and the fact that I'd made mama cry. Nobody cared when they made me cry. Nobody cared when I was shivering and alone in my drafty room wanting a hug or even a pat on the arm. Nobody cared when I was sick from the baby or tired or even about the little pains I'd been feeling off and on all day.

Everything was happening so fast in my head but moving so slow on the outside. I reached out to papa's worktable and grabbed the closest object. That's when time speeded up and his hand was flying at me now with the speed and force of a human jackhammer. I guess it was all the hormones they talk about pregnant women having that made me move, although I felt like I had turned that pity party in my head into a shield. I think I was acting more to save myself than any worry over the safety of the baby, truth be told.

I knocked papa's big paw down with one hand and struck at it with the tool in my other hand. It goes to show you just how wrong someone can be in the heat of the moment when they're not looking around carefully. I mean, there wasn't much I could do to be helpful with my normal chores, but I hadn't neglected papa's tools, especially since he needed them to work on whatever was under that sheet for the baby. So just like always, I kept them nice and sharp and clean for him. Goes to show what mama and papa knew, calling me lazy. Of course, that was little consolation to papa now, what with his hand pinned to the table and all.

At some point mama had stopped her little tirade, because she came running out when she heard all the shouting and screaming in the workshop. The shouting was papa, just as crazy as you like, standing there shaking his free fist and describing all sorts of ugly things he was gonna do with that fist to make me sorry I'd ever been born. The screaming was me. I mean, I'd killed plenty of critters but I'd never seen so much blood before, at least not like that--gurgling and spurting like one of those fountains in front of the fancy buildings that I saw once on a school trip to the big city.

Papa was just breathing heavily now; noisy, but no more shouting. Mama wouldn't stop yelling and pointing and coming at me. She threw the library book and began waving around a pan--her favorite heavy iron cooker. I couldn't move too fast in any direction so the book hit me square in the belly. I shuffled toward the back wall, realizing that soon I'd run out of space and one of mama's wild swings with that pan was gonna connect, even with her lousy aim. But I knew my aim was better, since papa made me practice over and over again, whether it was in the shed or on the lake or out hunting in the field.

I grabbed another tool off the workbench and waited. Mama was growing tired and I was feeling jittery. She jumped in with a big swing with that big pan and I made my move. Papa should have been proud of the way I set my target. It only took the one blow with the hammer to bring mama down. I looked back at papa to see if he'd seen. By now he'd sunk to his knees, his hand pinned over his head on the workbench, blood pumping more slowly now. He'd gone all quiet and glassy-eyed, but he was looking at me just the same. I was feeling a bit proud and a bit sick, all rolled up tight together like tangled twine. Since I couldn't figure what to do next, I put down the hammer and went inside the house.

At the kitchen table I helped myself to some warm brownies and cold milk and tried to figure out what I should do next. Turns out that first part was the easiest. Always is, mama would say. Once you get yourself in a mess, you always look back and wonder why you did this or that and you curse yourself and maybe some others for making it so easy for you. Though I didn't feel it was right to blame myself fully. I mean, I came from their union; I was their flesh and blood. Everything I was and did started with them, didn't it?

I thought about that some more and that's when the idea hit me. The perfect way to make the things that happened and the thing that was gonna happen any day now work together like they were all part of a larger plan. It was the only way to show everyone how much I'd learned. Then they'd have to agree I'd done right by my parents, even if I was the one that had first brought them such shame and then brought them to their early and unexpected demise.

First stop was papa's workshop. I tried not to look at the pool of blood on the workbench, or the splatters on the nearby wall, or papa's body, huddled under the bench with his arm raised like he had an urgent question for the teacher or something. I tried to ignore mama in a heap by the back wall, book and frying pan on either side of her with her own little halo of blood setting on the smooth concrete floor.

I waddled past all that and pulled the sheet off the present. As I suspected, it was a wooden cradle, carved smooth out of a large chunk of wood from one of those trees that fell in the late summer storms we had this year. Papa had just started to carve out the rockers on the bottom, but mama had already stenciled a design across the top and padded it with cotton batting and a tiny quilt in colors to match the stencil.

I got a little blubbery, thinking about how maybe they did love me or, if not me, my baby. Why couldn't they have said something? Why couldn't things have been different? Why did I feel like they were making this beautiful thing as another way to torture me? All the hard work and sacrifice and *blah blah blah* I would have had to listen to from them for the rest of their lives. I wiped my nose and shrugged it off. Can't make changes to a thing once it's gone beyond its end.

The unfinished rocker would be the perfect manger. I almost wished papa hadn't done such a fine job, so it looked a little more rough and antique-like. Right now it was as fancy and sturdy as any of those things you could buy down at the Woolworth's or through the Sears and Roebuck catalog. But it was there and it was mine and I pulled and pushed on it till I got it out into the yard. Then I took a break for another one of those brownies.

Next came the setting. I never took an art class, but I was pretty tickled by that backdrop. I used a big piece of old plywood papa kept out behind the house, and painted it black as a night without a moon, and dotted some tiny white stars around on it. Then I pasted on the big star of Bethlehem made out of some tinfoil so it was shiny. Then I propped it up behind that manger-crib and pushed some big rocks behind it so it'd stay in place.

I needed a break after all that physical stuff. My back was hurting and my feet were aching and the baby was making some feeble protest in my belly. I rewarded myself with another brownie. I figured it was ok seeing as how it was about lunchtime by then. I sat for a while staring at the clean dishes mama had left to dry next to the sink. Thinking I should get up and dry them and put them away. But I just sat there for a while longer, staring. I finally got up, grabbed some linens from the closet, and sat down at the sewing machine to get to work.

When I finished, I felt a little better because I knew mama would have been proud. I hauled my triumph out to the workshop and placed the pile carefully away from any of the bloody areas, even though by now they were setting up pretty good.

I decided to start with papa, figuring I'd have more energy in the beginning of it all. It took a good amount of tugging to get the wood chisel out of his hand. After it popped free he slid to the floor like a puppet with cut strings. I dragged him a little way away from the mess before I got him dressed up. Then I grabbed hold and slid him across the floor pretty easy till we got to the door.

Now's when I'd be working off that brownie. I heaved and ho'd him from left to right across the yard to where I'd set up the manger and the backdrop. Good thing I had thought ahead and set up that display in the middle of the yard, so it wasn't too far from either the workshop or the house. And even though I hadn't quite planned out all the next part, it turned out the rough flax shepherd's cape I made papa was pretty easy for hiding the dirt he collected as I pushed and shoved him into place.

I rolled him over and propped him up on his knees next to that manger, but his hands wouldn't cooperate so good to move into a prayer position. I tugged and pushed and set his arms out till his hands stayed palms flat together and propped up on the manger. Then I had to take another rest.

For months and months now that baby had been as quiet as you please. I figured it was hibernating and saving up all its strength for when it got dragged into the world and had to deal with terrified me and holier-than-thou mama and papa. Today of all days that little bastard decided to start putting up a fuss, and I was in no mood to fight any more family battles.

Turned out I wasn't done struggling with mama yet.

When I finally gave up on getting that baby to stop pushing and shoving I went back out to the workshop. I almost set to washing up the area where papa had been 'cause he hated when his workshop was messy and it was smelling a lot like wet pennies out there. But I had another job to do first so I made my way over to mama and grabbed hold of her arms.

No amount of tugging or pushing would get her going at the start. I set my feet, I tried rocking her, I just didn't have a lot of leverage with all my extra weight up front fighting me like it had a mind of its own. After a while it seemed to me maybe *mama* was the one who shoulda laid off the brownies and the other sweet treats she thought fit to deny me.

Finally I found an old rod in the corner and wedged that under her and heaved myself on top of it to get her body rocking a bit. Took me near an hour to get her across the floor and all dressed up, but then I had a little dilemma. I didn't want to drag her across the yard and get her pretty white outfit all dirty.

There was nothing around me in the workshop to help out. I went into the house and looked around. The towels were too threadbare and we only took baths, so no shower curtain. My sheets were too thin to be reliable. I walked to their room and stopped outside the door with my hand raised to knock, out of habit. Then I shook my head at my silly self and turned the knob to go inside.

I could probably count on one hand the number of times I'd stepped foot inside that room. It was a close space with the hand-me-down furniture that was too large to fit comfortably, and it was dark and still and tidy and eerie. Mama had made the bed up real tight and it seemed a shame to untuck the coverlet and sheets and lay them down out in the yard, but it had to be done.

On the way through the kitchen I caught a glance at the clock and was shocked at how late it was getting. I needed to get a move on so I could finish up and come up with a plan for the evening. Couldn't very well have brownies for dinner, could I?

I set the sheets out like a pathway. Too bad the yard was nice and flat and I couldn't roll mama into position. Instead I used that rod to get her into place and then dragged her along those sheets and wrestled her into place next to papa. It took even more struggle than with papa to get her hands fixed like his, but then I smoothed out her dress and folded that flap of skin on her head back into place from where I'd hit her with the hammer. I thought maybe I'd get a little rag to clean the dried blood off papa's hand and arm and off mama's face where it'd run all down, but when I straightened up the first big pain hit.

I likened it to mama actually making contact with that big heavy pan of hers, but hitting at me from the inside. It was different than all the pains from before, though. They hurt all right, but there wasn't the same kind of menace in them. This felt like it meant to finish me off and take joy in the course of it.

I was already bent over, so when the next pain hit I dropped to my knees. Anybody passing by would have seen me kneeling there between papa and mama and thought we were practicing our own Christmas play. Somewhere in between the grunting and breathing out and clenched teeth I realized I hadn't made myself a nativity outfit. With papa and mama the obvious Joseph and Mary (even though it was me who was bringing forth the child), where did I fit in?

No time to think too much about it, though, because the next pain felt like everything that was inside of me was trying to get out. I'm pretty sure I was screaming, but when I woke up it was that early evening time when the sun was still out playing but quickly gathering up his stuff to go inside, and everything was quiet.

I rolled to my side and could feel the damp between my legs and under my legs and I sat up to see a big, dark pool under my cold, still baby. He looked so much like a doll that I didn't even think to cry, just wiped him a little on my dress and tucked him in real good under that blanket in the crib-manger.

When I stood up I was woozy and chilled, and must have been quite a sight 'cause from out of nowhere it seemed the neighbors began gathering around and gawking and crying out. But no one came too close and I just kept getting colder and I figured it was because I'd stopped all the running around I'd been doing. Now that the baby was out there was no need to keep that internal furnace going, so maybe I was going to have to go inside and find a blanket.

That's when I noticed that papa's hair was turning white, and despite the evening starting to set in, everything around seemed to look lighter and clean, like the whole world was being bleached. I looked up to the sky, and watched the snowflakes swirling down right out of the depths of heaven. Just like it was in all of those Christmas carols, and those holiday movies they showed on the television each year.

I spread out my arms and twirled around, blinking snowflakes out of my eyelashes. The neighbors just kept standing and staring and not a one of them bothered to say what a nice job I'd done with the decorating. Or even how sorry they were, that even though they were all right there in the nativity, I didn't really have my papa or mama or baby any more and I was all alone on Christmas Eve.

Well I had more pride in myself than any of them could take away. I stopped twirling and turned to face them all.

"Si-lent night. Ho-ly night…"

Most of them were shaking their heads and clucking their tongues. The snow was coming down harder but I kept singing, even when I noticed some of them had gone back into their homes and put on their heavy jackets and then come back on out to watch me shiver my way through my song.

The youngest Denby boy, the one everyone called "touched," started to sing along with me before someone elbowed him hard and then shushed up his crying. So it was just me again, singing my whole life's worth into that one song, with no horns or strings or a huge chorus of people that you could imagine holding hands and going around the whole of the world like they was giving it a big hug.

"Sleep in heav-en-ly peace…"

My body was numb and my voice was quavering but I finished it off pretty nice before the cars with the sirens roared into view, churning the deepening snow into something wet and dirty. Men jumped out of the cars with their guns at the ready and the neighbors moved out of the way just enough to get out of the line of fire.

I was cold and hungry and tired and dizzy on the outside, but that carol was echoing around on the inside of my head, drowning out my pains and making me smile. That's when the sheriff's men told me to drop to the ground.

I didn't want any trouble. I'd never really wanted any trouble. Just a moment or two of my very own to feel like I was someone special. Not special quite like this, but I did what they said. I dropped to the ground.

On my back.

I smiled up at the sky, full of flakes falling like manna. I could feel the cushion of them underneath, like God had left a pillow on the ground that was just for me. I spread my limbs wide and fanned them up and down, up and down. I imagined each snowflake was a kind and loving kiss from above. Soon my limbs grew heavy and I slowed down, then I stopped moving altogether. With one last sigh I felt warm, and wanted, and at peace.

I was finally somebody's angel.

Fallen Leaves

I was running late, so I turned down the alley to take the shortcut. It wasn't the best route--even in daylight--but especially now as the sun began to set and everything from the mountains to down here in the valley was bathed in a rosy glow. At the mouth of the alley, hookers and addicts were beginning to congregate. Some of them I knew from my job as a social worker, but I kept my head down and nodded discreetly as I passed.

After a while I realized I could no longer hear their hushed voices. The silence was eerie and I began to walk more quickly, aware of growing ominous shapes and shadows. Then I began to run a little--a ridiculous lope, actually--which turned out to be another bad idea. Halfway down the alley I twisted my ankle when one of my pencil-thin heels caught in a microscopic gap in the pavement.

Damn new shoes! Why had I let the saleswoman talk me into what was fashionable instead of practical? My calves didn't look any slimmer in the thin heels than the wedges, I thought, as I was forced to stop and rub and rotate my ankle slowly. Although the peach shoes *did* match my dress, which contrasted nicely with my brown skin (I tried to soothe myself with vanity). I looked down at my arms, which were normally smooth but had suddenly become mottled with goose pimples. My hands had been sweaty from clutching my purse, but now they were cooled by the evening breeze. I realized I was getting cooled, too, as the darkness settled in quickly for the night and the temperature began to drop.

What had I been thinking, telling my date I'd meet him at the restaurant? True, he didn't know where I lived in case things went horribly wrong, but how much safer was what I was doing? If my car weren't in the shop, if I'd planned ahead and arranged a cab, if I'd taken the longer route to get downtown. One less "if" and maybe I wouldn't have to alternate between rubbing my bare arms for warmth (spaghetti straps to show off all my hard work at the gym, but I'd run out without a jacket!) and rubbing my throbbing ankle.

Well it was only going to get colder and later, so I decided to try walking. I slowly straightened and lowered my leg, inch by inch till I could just feel my shoe touch the pavement. As I shifted more and more weight onto my ankle I could feel a slight twinge and I pulled back. This was no good. I looked behind me, but the alley curved slightly and I could no longer see the night crowd at its entrance. Ahead of me I could see large shadows and the occasional sounds of downtown carried on a breeze.

This was silly. All of the action was downtown, a mere five or six blocks from where I was standing. All of the businesses that backed onto the alley were closed for the evening. I was going to have to help myself and do it quickly in order to stay warm. I straightened my leg, shifted my weight onto the ankle, stood up straight, and crumpled at the sudden roar.

The sound was impossibly large and everywhere all at once. In confusion I fell against the curb next to a *No Parking* sign. The sound stopped as quickly as it had started. Once I realized it wasn't some cosmic bellow at my stupidity, I pulled myself up by the edge of the sign and tried to make sense of what had happened. The sound was familiar--something I normally associated with crisp morning air on the weekends. It suddenly came to me--who could be using a leaf blower in an alley in the dark?

Once on my feet I looked around. Up ahead and off to the left I could see a tall man walking away from me, now turning the leaf blower on and off rhythmically as he moved into one of the loading dock areas that backed onto the alley. I crossed to the other side of the alley and began to limp quickly toward downtown. As I passed the point where the man had turned, I heard a loud thump. My head turned involuntarily and I could see the man crouching, almost catlike, on the metal apron of one of the loading bays. There were no stairs or ladders that I could make out--he must have jumped the six feet up to the landing! He turned his torso slightly toward me and began to straighten up. I wasn't interested in meeting up with anyone that creepy and that strong in a dark, deserted alley, so I limped faster, almost hopping along the road.

Finally I could see the cross street at the end of the alley. It too, was an office and warehouse strip that was empty at this hour, but two blocks beyond that was lots of wine and fine dining *and warmth*, I thought as I could feel my jaws quiver in a first wave of teeth chattering. I passed another truck bay where a man wielded a leaf blower. I knew the city was fanatical about leaves now that we were entering the rainy season, but it seemed odd for private companies to –

I stopped suddenly. It finally hit me what was really so out of place. There were no trees in, or on either side of, the alley! The two truck bays were long and separated by a wall, but both belonged to the same warehouse, so the two men with the leaf blowers clearly worked for the same company. But what were they doing?

The man looked up and saw me watching him. He paused briefly then moved out into the alley in front of me and continued to blow debris back toward a large dumpster in the truck bay. Trash, I thought. With all of the manufacturing and offices around here, who knew what kind of stuff would show up and collect in the alley? I thought about the crew I'd passed on the way in. Cigarette butts, bottles, needles, condoms. Almost in response to my musings, a stray scrap of something twirled away from the man and across my feet. It was large and pale, and, despite the absence of trees around, looked like a leaf that'd been bleached in the sun. But clouds had dominated for the past few weeks, so how could that be?

I bent over and picked up the leaf for a closer look, only vaguely aware that the man in front of me had turned off his machine. The leaf was thin and fragile so I held it by the edges and examined its shape and veins. In my long-gone Girl Scout days (and maybe with a lot more light) I'd know which many-lobed variety this was, but it was absolutely foreign to me now. I marveled at how easily it flopped and folded, and the texture appeared to be different and darker on the other side. I turned the leaf over for a closer look, and screamed.

* * *

I remembered stopping one day to hear a street preacher talk about the sins of us all, and how our fallen souls were in need of mending. Mending made me think of clothes, not spirituality. I was, in fact, on my way to do some shopping, no doubt sinning and contributing to the soulless apathy that he warned against.

I made my way through the sparse crowd and caught his eye before crossing the street--the street that I could now see spread before me at the end of the block. The Tree of Life, he kept saying. We are all leaves on the Tree of Life. The tree of unending sustenance and happiness. And once we fall from the tree, because of the natural decay of our frail, human form or, more likely, through the degradation of our body and spirit through sin, we can never be reclaimed. In the case of the former, we give selflessly of ourselves, even in death, by feeding the tree and nurturing the continuity of the human race. In the case of the latter, we lie shriveled and spotted, diseased, as the roots of the tree shrink away from the ravages of evil.

He promised to purge our evil thoughts and *stay our hands to stop our evil deeds*. And here I held his solution in the palm of my own hand.

Because it wasn't a leaf at all. It was the thin cross-section of a human hand, soft and delicate and easily able to float away on the barest breath.

In front of me, the man shook his head, smiled, and began walking toward me. At some point during my reverie he had put down the leaf blower and was holding a muddy shovel. Except that when he moved under one of the scarce streetlights I could see that the shovel was wet, but not glistening with mud.

I opened my mouth, but this time nothing came out but a squeak. I began to move backwards, hopping, keeping my eyes on the man in front of me who did not increase his pace and did not stop smiling. I opened my mouth again.

"Help," I cried weakly. "Help me," I cried a little louder. I grew more confident. I was only two blocks from downtown now. Surely I could yell loud enough for someone to hear me.

I took a deep breath and opened my mouth again to yell, but faltered as the man stopped walking and smiled even wider. I continued my backward hop until I could feel every hair on my body stand on end, as if trying to secede. The tension was like the crackle before a lightning strike and I looked briefly skyward, waiting for the bolt. Instead I felt a tug of air from behind me and realized too late, even as I opened my mouth to its widest, that my scream would be forever drowned out by the thunder of the leaf blower roaring to life behind me.

Does Your Mother Know?

It was the strangest thing any of them had ever asked him.

"Why are you doing this?" "What do you want from me?" "How can you live with yourself?" "What did I ever do to you?" Sure, he had heard all of those. But this?

He actually stopped in mid-stroke, merely grazing her arm instead of giving it the hefty chop meant to separate it from the rest of her body.

"What did you say?" he squeaked.

"Does your mother know?!" she screamed. "Does your mother know how flaccid and weak and cowardly you are, you sick, perverted fu—"

Thunk.

Before he even knew what he was doing, he cleaved her head. He watched sadly as the blood and tissue that didn't splatter onto the walls dribbled down into a wet pile on the plastic laid out on the floor.

Anger never pays, he thought, shaking his head. It had always been his weakness, that short fuse. He wasn't sure where it originated. His mother never displayed any emotion, and his father was never around enough for him to know for certain.

Damn. He had been looking forward to spending a lot of time with this one, savoring each squirm and squirt till the end. Now his frustration had gotten the better of him, and it was too soon to go out and get another one.

Really. The idea that he gave a rat's ass whether or not his mother knew. Had she ever known anything about him? Hadn't she always been pushing him away, out the door, out of her life, so she could sneak men in by the back door, the windows, the garage, while her husband--his father--was away at work?

Wasn't she the one who ignored the notices from the school about his delinquency, promised the neighbors his labor on the weekends when they accused him of having something to do with their pets going missing, and let him see or read or do whatever he wanted just so he was out of sight, out of her hair, and off her list of things for which she was responsible?

He laughed. The sound was forced and too loud. It had been a long time since something had annoyed him so profoundly. Now he had that question floating around in his head, mocking him, taunting him. The fact that he didn't really have an answer annoyed him even further.

He began pacing the room. He accidentally kicked a part of the broken skull and crunched down on a chip of bone. He looked down at his goopy boots. He laughed again, with more genuine feeling.

What *would* his mother think? If she saw him living in his basement apartment with the (currently plastic-coated) red shag rug and black walls and the smell--that smell of things overly washed and insufficiently clean? What would she think of his empty refrigerator, his empty checking account, his empty life? What would she say about his attempts to please someone, anyone? To live up to some standard that he set for himself because no one else in his life seemed to care enough to raise the bar for him?

Would she say anything? Do anything? Would she even listen long enough to understand what kind of a man he had become? After hours agonizing over it, he decided to take action. It was time to find his mother and find out.

* * *

"It's me," he answered when she made a cautious inquiry at her front door.

It had taken him a few days to track her down. She had been moving around frequently in recent years, and never bothered to put him on her list of people to notify.

"Me who?" she asked in return.

He grimaced. "Your son."

He waited, picturing her safely inside, considering her options. Although he had never raised his voice or hand in defiance to her, she had always walked around him carefully, as if he were a rare specimen or volatile compound that could be spooked or triggered into something uncontainable and disastrous.

After an eternity he heard a click, and the door opened a crack. He saw one of his mother's bright green eyes peering through the opening, and her questioning look flipped his switch. He shoved the door inward with both hands, and the force knocked her back into the living room. She lay whimpering, holding a couple of fingers across the bridge of her nose to stop the bleeding from where the edge of the door cut her.

He moved quickly inside, picked her up from the floor and dropped her into one of the antique wing chairs she loved so much. So much that she told him from the first day she brought them home he was never allowed to sit in them, touch them, or look at them. So much that when the puppy he had craved and begged and waited many months to own finally made its floppy slobbery appearance in their home, but disappeared suddenly and unexplainably after two days, he knew the dog had somehow desecrated those damn chairs.

He smiled in genuine satisfaction when she accidentally smeared some blood on the chair arm while trying to pull herself up and away from him. He dragged an ottoman in front of her and sat uncomfortably close, pinning her arms to the arms of the chair with his hands.

"The entire time I was growing up we never seemed to have many reasons to get to know each other, outside of the fact that you were my mother and I was your son," he said. "But today someone made me wonder why that is. Or how it is that two people who at one time were literally inseparable, now exist so wildly apart from one another."

He lifted one hand to her face and turned it toward him, forcing her to make eye contact. "So I think it's time for us to have our bonding moment, our memory-making mother-son conversation, our soul-baring episode. Mother, let's talk."

* * *

It took hours, but he walked her through each lovely detail of every single one. He started with the thrill of choosing them. Of knowing the look he wanted without being able to define it as a type. Instead, it was about how the eyebrows lifted or how the mouth could move to smile or smirk with ease. It was in the bearing--

quietly confident, oddly present while pushing a background persona. It was in the eyes of tinted, unknowable glass.

It was her, he realized with a start.

This cold, alabaster being sitting before him with her haughty, unbreakable will and concern more for the appearance of her damaged nose than her son's sudden and violent re-entry into her life. *She was his ideal victim.*

He felt a flush of warmth. He was excited and aroused, but nothing Oedipal, he reasoned. No, he didn't want his mother. He wanted to destroy her. He wanted to break her façade and leave her open and vulnerable and broken beyond repair like so many before.

He continued his narrative for her, moving on to how he hunted. How he enjoyed being a silent and secretive spectator to their lives, watching them in their moments of banality and beauty until he confirmed for himself that they were right. Then he logged their movements and habits until he found the right time or place to overwhelm them with his height and his strength and stuff them unconscious into the trunk of his car. He didn't take them home right away. Instead he liked to drive around, tempting fate and enjoying the danger of possible discovery.

As much as he enjoyed the foreplay, nothing compared to the state of capture. He replayed the delectable sound of each slice, each begging word, each invective, each scream. He described the smell as it changed from a fresh tang to a stale, coppery stink. He even walked his mother through each journey with each piece of each girl as he scattered them to the winds. There was power in knowing they were out there, everywhere, surrounding him, silent and subjugated.

His mother appeared to be listening to every word, but her face was impassive. He might as well have been talking about buying groceries, going to the dry cleaner, or been reading her a story from one of those erudite, dispassionate news magazines she had always favored.

This had been his life, he remembered. Nothing moved her, either to anger or praise. Straight As, failing grades, making the team, losing a job, all were met with the same stony countenance, as if everything about him was inconsequential. He was frustrated. He mattered. What he did mattered to him. And it mattered to all of those girls and their friends and their families.

Maybe she didn't believe him. He gave more details about the trophies he kept. The most memorable trait of each girl that he could enshrine in his atrocious archives in order to visit and revisit each one of them. Bloody eyelashes, rings from severed fingers, a lock of hair he'd cut off and used to gag its unusually loud owner, a belly button ring with belly button still attached.

Again, he was excited in the retelling, able to relive each glorious accomplishment. The extreme peril coupled with an even bigger payoff, the knowledge that he was the only one in the world to have done what he had done and taken what he had taken. The rest of his life, up to and surrounding this, was at best average. This was something he excelled at. Surely she could see it.

He waited for horror, disgust, fear. Anything to signal that she heard and understood and appreciated the depths of his disease. When it was clear he had nothing else to add, she closed her eyes, as if lost in thought. Moments passed and he felt himself growing anxious, which made him angry.

"So how many does that make?" she finally asked.

He did the math in his head. "Twelve."

She nodded, just barely. Still no sign of emotion on her face. He shifted on the ottoman, acutely aware now of how close he was to her. He couldn't remember the last time he'd been able to smell the sandalwood musk she always wore, or to see how time had slowly etched canyons into her neck and around her mouth. As he studied her face her eyes popped open, dull and unfocused, looking at some point beyond his left shoulder.

"I had fifteen by the time I was your age," she said. Her eyes refocused and she looked straight at him, into him, for the first time in a long time. And then she smiled. A genuine self-satisfied smile he had never seen before. And never wanted to see again.

* * *

All of those men. All of those times he thought she loved them more than she could ever love him. Well, in a way it was true. She hadn't wanted him, hadn't wanted to get married, but he and his father were the perfect way for her to stay safe. No one would fear or suspect a young wife and mother. People were so stupid in their willingness to believe in the greater good.

So those men came, one after one, like willing sheep to her slaughter. But it was never about him versus them. It was never about competing with them for her attention and affection, as he had always believed. She loved the power she took them from them, the way she could prey and feed on them one after another after another. They filled a chasm no filial bond could ever match. His mother had been as driven then as he was now, and would have continued if her charms hadn't aged along with the rest of her. The question was whether some part of him knew.

Was he his mother's son because of something dark and rotten that was built into his being, or because he had seen or heard or smelled something she had done that awoke a bestial desire deep within him? Something that lurked in everyone but was only triggered in a few?

Well, he'd never know now. Once again his temper had gotten the best of him. It started with that laugh, then came the taunting and mocking and questioning of his ability to match his dear mother at their shared craft.

But it was when she questioned his choices, his methods, and his celebration of his skills that he choked back the questions he had for her and choked the life right out of her.

At first he had wanted to keep her eyes, so she could "watch" as he surpassed her kill count, but he figured they'd soon become smelly, meaningless blobs and he had enough regular cleanup to do as it was. Instead he took her hands, and mounted them carefully in a box lined with the fabric from those stupid wing chairs. The rest of her body he scattered in the woods behind her house before burning the place to the ground.

He wondered how things might have been different if his father had stuck around. True, he was already in his late teens at the time his father walked out on them, and undoubtedly the damage had already been done, but could he have learned to be different? Tried harder to be normal?

It was too late now and, when he thought about it, he didn't care that much. He was who he was and he liked things the way they were. His mother's hands sat in the box on the mantle and he sat on his couch, formulating a plan. It all felt right, and that was good enough for him.

He understood at last that it didn't matter whether his mother had blessed him with nature or (lack of) nurture. She left him with a legacy, a gift that he was still free to share, and was now inspired to share even more.

His mother made number thirteen for him. To beat her count he needed at least three more before his birthday next month.

He had to get busy.

The Corner of My Eye

It is better here in the hospital. The smell is clean and safe, the surfaces soft. There is comfort in the squeak of shoes on floors slick with lemon disinfectant and conditioning wax. The chairs are overstuffed and inviting; you can sink into a womb world that holds you close and echoes the sound of your own pounding heartbeat.

I often forget the unhappy winter wind outside. It is always summer in here. The lights are bright, the mood is yellow, and laughter and music are everywhere. It has been a long time since I have seen the darkness or heard the inner knocking of my fear.

I used to be cold all the time. Inside, where no sun or blanket or even the biggest bonfire could penetrate and bring me back to normal. Here, the heat from the vents is so thick you can almost taste the particles carried helplessly along on the path through the ducts. It makes me sleepy and empties my head of the bad thoughts.

That is why I am here. Not for the thoughts themselves, but for how they made me feel. What they made me do. It seems like a lifetime ago, now. I was a different person then. I cringe when I think about how weak I used to be. I talk about that a lot with my nurse and my doctor.

My nurse is my one connection to the outside world. No one comes to visit me any more, so she is my reminder that everything everywhere is not so insulated and safe and muted. She has a life-loving, inelegant laugh. For her I am able to find those things worth smiling about. I don't talk to her about the dark things, for fear that her laugh will turn nervous and insincere and then fade away, like it always did with the people I knew before I came here.

Her joy is the perfect counterpoint to my doctor's anxious whisper. Although he speaks the words like someone with a special knowledge and power, I have figured out his secret. He knows words, no matter how small, have the weight to unstitch raw and jagged psyches. He wields them with great care, out of what I first thought was a conscious display of self-control. Now I know it is out of reverence. Like so many of us, he is a puppet to words. *They* possess the knowledge and power, not him.

My doctor is cautious with me because I tell him the truth. Some of the others in here lie; they are afraid no one will believe them. I tried talking to them, to let them know this was a safe place and the monsters could not come here, but they always ran away. I think it is because they know. They have experienced the same things for themselves. They just don't want to believe they could end up like me. Nothing is crazier than the truth, though. Nothing is as terrifying as real life.

I was normal once. I went to school, got a job, had a family. I worried about bills and debt and the rising cost of gasoline. I worried about pension plans, the stock market, and identity theft. I worried about the computer on my desk, the computer in my car, and the computer that was my personal digital assistant. I worried about the headaches and the chest pain and the doctor telling me to stop worrying "or else."

It started with the little things. That's always the way, it seems. The little things grow into bigger things until you are surrounded by menacing towers of doom and you can't see a way out. But the little things didn't grow bigger for me. They just grew into more little things. I was a hoarder of mental minutiae. Bit by bit by bit it all expanded until I felt I was drowning, and all of a sudden I realized it was too late to escape.

You want to know what they are, don't you? You want to know why I am here, and what it is that I did. You are imagining the kinds of things that put people here, and you're waiting in anticipation to hear my own particular horror story.

Fact is, you already know about the little things. You are just too scared to put a name to them. To recognize them as a pattern, like I did. To admit there is a conspiracy being waged against you, a war of terror, a personal vendetta waged by God or aliens or the universe, depending on what you believe.

It does not help to tell yourself you are a good person. Good people meet bad fates. Good people are harassed and tortured on a regular basis. Good people die every day. That has nothing to do with it. It is time for you to acknowledge the darker side of life. The evil twin. The run of bad luck. You must dispose of the naive idea that things get worse before they get better.

Sometimes things just get worse.

That is what I tell my doctor when we talk. Now he's afraid to ask more. Sometimes he's afraid to even whisper those everyday greetings and soothing words required of him. I know he's afraid to discover what it is

I have seen. Afraid that if I speak the words aloud--describe the fear in detail--the fear receives new life and moves on to find another home. He should know it doesn't work that way. We each already carry our own burden. How strong we are inside determines how long it takes the load to break us down.

I've written them down, however. The little things. When I'm feeling a little stronger I will make my doctor listen so he can understand. Like you understand. I can share them with you. The little things that choked the air and light from my life until I had no other choice but to do what I did to stop them all. I know you understand, because at any given time one of you is mere moments away from becoming just like me.

Everyone has his or her special fear. Most of us fear many things, but usually these things can be traced to a primal, overarching fear. I have always been afraid of dying. Dying in my sleep, dying in a fiery car accident, drowning, choking, falling down the stairs and breaking my neck. No matter the method, I do not want to go. Not yet.

Of course those are random events – unpredictable, blameless. The things that really terrify me are the ways to die that are not so random; the deliberate, methodical killing, or the frenzied, directed attack. The kind of death where someone or something consciously decides to remove me from the world. Some deeper part of me knows that is the way I am destined to go.

I tried to laugh it off as paranoia. I reexamined my deeds and my life to see if there was cause for concern. There was nothing obvious, but the feeling persisted. And then I started to see the signs.

There were those times I swore I saw the bright enamel of a toothy grin as I lowered a shade or closed the blinds. Even in the midst of denial, I wondered if I had remembered the security bar on that slider door leading out to the deck, or the tricky latch on the bathroom window down the hall. You know, the one window of the entire house in the blind spot from the neighbor's view. The window in the dip of the hill and surrounded by overgrown vegetation that was always on my weekend list of things to do, but never seemed quite as important.

Certainly not as important as enjoying a refreshing swim in the pool after a long, hot morning of loafing in the sun reading the paper. Isn't that what weekends were made for? They were not made for feeling, with each lap, that there were extra waves in the pool. Not made for feeling like someone was swimming just behind me and slowly reaching out to make contact. Certainly not made for feeling, when I was blinded with fatigue and chlorine and reaching for the towel I had placed on the edge of the pool, that a hand was waiting to slink out and push my head down and hold it under the water.

Try telling an idea like that to your friends, or your mate. Normally so understanding, nodding their heads with sympathy when you spill your darkest fears, but I could swear I saw them wink to each other as I was turning away.

Unfortunately, it wasn't just at home. At work, at the movies, out to dinner, I knew I saw a rustling of the leaves near my car as I opened the door. I started to park in the middle of the lot so there was nowhere for someone or something to hide, but then I was surrounded by so many cars and the shadows between and under each of those cars. What do you do if a hand slips out from underneath one of the many dark areas and grabs you, slices you, drags you down?

I avoided empty bathrooms and hallways. I only ate with others around, and I confined my extracurricular activities to the daylight, so I could retreat to the safety of my home before darkness fell.

You just never know.

That's when I became obsessive about using the electronic security gate across the driveway. But could that have been a shadow slipping by, impossibly thin and fast, making its way toward the one door I've left open as I tend to the lock on the gate?

Inside, things seemed untouched, normal. The lights were on as I had left them. A gust of wind stirred ashes in the fireplace and leaves on the balcony into a synchronized, swirling dance. I hurried past, afraid that I might lose focus and become careless.

No dark corners waited in the other rooms because by now my family had left me and the rooms were empty and I always left all of the lights on. No shadows pressed themselves against the windows. The hallway was an open passage to the oasis of the bedroom, where I seemed to be spending more and more time alone with my fears.

I tried to relax in my home office (I spent almost all of my time at home now, it was easier to control my surroundings), but I saw the stalking, stiff-legged gait of a spider coming toward me. I had just bug-bombed the house because the little suckers terrify me. I turned quickly and there was nothing there, but I began to wonder if there were armies of spiders or ghostly husks of former spiders seeking revenge. My skin crawled and I needed something to make me feel better.

Despite where I found myself, emotionally, psychologically, I did not consider myself one to bow easily to fear (extreme unease, yes). I needed a shower, I took a shower. The warmth, the smell of the citrus soap, the massage of my fingers on my scalp, all helped to allay my previous concerns. If only I hadn't thought, just for a moment, as I rinsed the shampoo from my head and soap from my face, that a finger--long and bony as a skeletal claw--was curling around the shower curtain in silent anticipation.

Time flew by, and I couldn't help feeling that the walk-in closet was deeper than I remembered. In fact, each day it seemed longer, stretching further into the darkness. There were not more clothes, just more murky space beyond them. It was certainly deep enough now to hide someone behind the clothes that seemed to shift and sway, long after I picked out my outfit for the day.

Weeks and months passed, and all of the little things continued to pile and pick and poke until I felt heavy and jumpy and raw all the time. I took a sabbatical from work because time on the computer distracted me from necessary periodic safety patrols. I had my groceries delivered because there were too many unknowns beyond the walls and the security gate. Summer brought with it endless days of sunshine and extreme heat outside, yet I constantly walked under shadowed skylights in the house, feeling chills that were only amplified when I looked out the windows and confirmed that, in fact, the sky was blue and clear and perfectly cloudless.

The light summer nights should have meant more comfort; fewer hours in which "incidents" could occur under cover of darkness. But as the world went dark, there was a period of time before the lights in the backyard would blaze to life. I huddled and waited until a greater fear of not knowing drove me from the bed and to the blinds. But there was nothing out there and nowhere to hide in that hundred-watt glare.

By the very end, it was constant. Although I had barricaded myself into a secure, well-lit room, my head was whipping from side to side with each imagined sighting of something that was never there.

I struggled for a while before I came up with the solution. It was one of those moments when you wonder why such an epiphany didn't come *before* the loss of family and friends and job and sleep. I mean, by now there was *nothing* I wanted to see head on, let alone in glimpses as I hurried from the security of one patrolled place to the next.

It was not an easy thing to carry out, even though on the face it was a flawlessly logical decision. It was precipitated by a bird flying into a window one day. A window no bird had ever flown into before, which made me wonder if the stakes had been raised. Was I now under intentional, active assault on all fronts by any and all comers? As the bird lay on the ground it looked in my direction, unseeing, before it stopped moving.

Unseeing.

It was clearly time to act. I hurried to the kitchen, opened the drawer, and carefully lifted out my first choice. It was freshly sharpened and gleaming with reflections of only me. I finally felt like I was on the path to safety.

I wondered whether I should move slowly or quickly, like the shadow beings that had been weighing on my mind and nerves for so many countless months. I was no longer as brave as I had once been. I no longer had the energy or will to fight the long fight. I was eager to be rid of the burden that I had carried with me for so long. So I moved quickly, bringing the weapon to both sockets before the pain could stay my hand.

* * *

It's time for my medication again. In the mornings they give me the tiny colored pills to keep me calm throughout the day. Nighttime is therapeutic, now.

That's when they give me the big white pills to help the holes to heal.

Yes, it is better here. No shadows, no slinking, no secrets. For the first time in a long time I feel relief rather than anxiety, anticipation rather than dread. I am much stronger now, and I look forward to each day's challenges as they come.

Ironic, really, how living in darkness has helped me to overcome my fear of it. But I am heartened by the fact that I made the choice myself. That I entered the unknown on my terms. I find the whole thing quite sensible. Others tend to disagree. I think this is my transition, however. This is a safe place that will ease me back to full health.

I think maybe I can convince my doctor to let me move on. To spread the word of hope to those of you who still have fear. It is peace beyond meditation, religion, or the power of positive thinking. It is action begetting enlightenment. I am living proof. There are always options. And now that I have found that peace, I can truly say I have found a better place.

I know you understand me – that you can relate. You've been there. You're there now. The headaches, chest pain, unsettled stomach. Worrying about the "what ifs" and wondering at what point they become the "whens".

But you can stop worrying. You, too, can be free of the anxiety that clouds your mind and crushes your spirit. We can talk about it, you and I. I can help you see how truly wonderful it is. I know it may not seem like it at first, but don't let the fear keep you from the best way to get back to you. You deserve it. You owe it to yourself and to those around you.

Look at me. I'm on the road to serenity and safety. The pain is gone. I can embrace the unknown without consequence. I have new insight to share with those who are despondent and drifting like I once was.

And all because I no longer worry about the things I used to see--out of the corner of my eye.

Down by the Sea

There is a shack on the beach made from the bones of the sea. It is a small shelter from the sand and wind, sitting safely above the roar of the waves, nestled in the curve of a ledge bristling with sea grapes.

As a child I visited the shack in the mornings with my grandfather and sat within its three slotted walls, made from the lost limbs of washed out, washed up trees. The roof boards came from crates or ships or perhaps other shacks sitting on the beaches of other seas.

I loved the secretive feel of the place. There was something profound about the serenity it offered. But my favorite part by far was the curtain of kelp, hanging down in long strands, blowing in the breeze like the princess's locks from my favorite fairy tale, "The Little Mermaid."

My mother read that story to me every night. She laughed at my questions about life underwater. She had never known a home other than the Midwestern suburb in which we lived. I told her when I grew up I would find a prince and have lots of children that could live on the land or in the sea. She laughed again and said she hoped my dream came true.

When she died, my father moved us back to his boyhood home on the coast to live with my grandfather. My grandmother had died a few years before and my grandfather was all alone. He and my father bonded in their grief and sense of isolation. I hid my sadness behind questions about whether mermaids and water witches really existed. My grandfather told me the only way to truly know was to find out for ourselves. We would walk across the dusty, two-lane road from home to the beach, and settle ourselves into the shack.

"Where does it come from?"

I could have been asking about the shack or the ocean or the sky or a barge on the water. Somehow my grandfather always knew, and always had an answer.

The ocean was made up of all the tears that had ever been, or would ever be shed. The sky came from wishes and hopes and dreams, which is why it was always changing colors and textures. The barges came from faraway places and carried secret treasures too fabulous for most people to ever see.

Then there was the shack. It had its own magic. It had been here since before my grandfather's grandfather, pieced together and repaired as needed for more than a century. When I was very young I could simply walk in through the open side that looked out onto the water. Once inside, the slope of the sand and the flat roof forced me to kneel or sit next to my grandfather, who always had to bend over and shuffle his way in.

We sat silently on the red wool blanket he brought for us to share, scanning the water that lay endlessly before us. Eventually my attention would wander. I'd watch the people jogging by, the seagulls scrabbling over treats left behind by summer vacationers, or the clouds of flies that lifted en masse from the sand as a wave washed over their resting spot. I scooted around uncomfortably on the blanket, rubbing at the backs of my legs where it scratched them. Still, my grandfather stared, nearly motionless, out to sea.

I ran off to play with my friends or go to school or whatever other life activity took me away until it was time for the sun to go down. Then I rejoined my grandfather, still sitting in the shack on the itchy, worn blanket where I had left him.

We watched the sun sink behind the water, dyeing the waves red and gold and deep, deep purple. Then we folded the blanket, climbed up the small dunes, and made our way back across the road to home.

Every day, for years, the routine was the same. I thought my grandfather sat on the beach to reflect upon his life, to mourn the loss of my grandmother (he was once again alone on this front; my father had remarried), or simply to stare, unthinking, into the blue-grey water. It wasn't until later I learned he was watching for something in particular.

It was the night of the ten-year anniversary of my grandmother's death. After dinner, my grandfather pushed himself away from the dining table, grabbed a sweater and the wool blanket, and walked out. My stepmother stared at the door for a few seconds, her eyes squinting and her lips pursing as if drawn together by the same string. I knew that look, and excused myself so I could slip into the hallway to spy before she could send me to my room.

"It's not natural!" she hissed in that urgent whisper she used when she didn't want anyone else to hear, but she wanted to make her point perfectly clear to my father.

"It's not like he's hurting anyone." My father stared down into his empty wineglass. His fingers twitched toward the bottle, but he would have to look up to safely grab and pour, and that left him vulnerable to my stepmother's stare.

"What about Renee? She spends so much time out there with him, sitting in that thing, participating in his weird vigil."

"Renee is fine," my father said, finally looking up and corralling the wine bottle.

He was protective of me; sensitive to any suggestion I was anything but okay. Even though she was now the mother I had known for half of my life, my stepmother became a stranger to me when she pushed my father about my wellbeing.

"I'm glad she likes spending time with my father," he said, concentrating on his glass. He lifted the bottle too quickly to pour, and the wine burst forth in red spurts, sprinkling the table with dark flecks that my father drew absently into a line with his finger.

"Besides, she's doing well in school, she has lots of friends. There's no problem here."

He sipped his wine and glanced toward the hallway. He knew I was there, but he always told me we had no secrets from each other.

"What about his stories? Those stories he used to tell you about the ocean? About how your mother died?"

My father swallowed quickly and placed his glass firmly on the table.

"That's enough. I'm sorry I even told you about any of that."

She started to protest, but he held up his hand.

"We're not talking about this any more because there's nothing to talk about. Leave it alone."

He grabbed his glass, got up from the table, and walked over to the large windows that looked out onto the shadows shifting across the road and the sand dunes.

Somewhere on the other side of those hills, my grandfather sat alone in the chill evening air, protected only by a skeletal box.

My stepmother cleared the table and leaned against the kitchen counter, her arms crossed, staring at my father's back as he sipped at the last of his wine. Despite his casual pose, the tension in his shoulders made it clear he was not to be approached.

I didn't know whose side to take. These days, the line between them seemed to appear more often and become more solid with each showing. My father was stubborn, unyielding, and moody. We had a good relationship, but I always felt there was some part of himself that he locked away from me, from everyone. My stepmother was open, affectionate, and, to my mind, needlessly overprotective.

Neither one of them moved or spoke for an eternity. I began to imagine what I might say or do to get them to look at each other, talk to each other, solve a problem that was bigger than themselves. Eventually I gave up hope and moved down the hallway to my room.

My grandfather never told me any stories about the sea. Just answers to my questions, or encouragement of my imaginings of the lives of mermaids and mermen. When I asked what he thought, he told me he only knew one true story of the sea, but that I wasn't old enough to hear it. By the time I was too old to be tucked in (and, presumably, old enough to be able to appreciate his story), I had forgotten about it.

Now I wondered if that tale related to what my stepmother said. What was so unnatural about his visits to the shore? If my grandmother's drowning was not accidental, what had happened? And why would my father have kept it from me?

The next day my grandfather did not seem surprised to find me waiting at the door for him instead of going surfing with my friends as I had been doing for the past few weeks. He handed me the blanket, smiled, and turned back into the kitchen where he grabbed random items and shoved them into a cloth bag.

"Rations," he answered my questioning look.

The morning fog was heavy at this time of year. From the top of the dunes, the water was invisible. The sky and the earth blurred into a grey void from which nothing could escape. We gave ourselves up to it, lowering our bodies into the misty soup and making our way to the shack.

Inside, our breathing put more curtains of fog between us. I would have thought I was alone except for the slight warmth and vague shape next to me on the blanket. The absence of the sand and water was disturbing. I felt we had entered another dimension and horrible things awaited us along the dreary path home.

"It will be coming soon, Renee," my grandfather said, as if reading my mind. The fog was lifting and there were hints of waves beyond the invisible sand.

His voice was even and resigned. I turned to see his face, but it was as if a veil had fallen once again between us. He stared ahead to where the water lay hidden.

"What's coming?"

Even as the words left my mouth I regretted the answer. *Any* answer. I wanted things to be the way they had always been. Ignorance is more than bliss. It is sanity.

"Our destiny is coming," he answered, turning to me.

The fog was dispersing quickly now, leaving us a chance at clarity.

"What happened to grandma?"

My grandfather's eyes filled with tears. He held on to them, though, just as he held onto his secret about the sea.

"It's not your time yet," he whispered.

"I'm sixteen! I'm old enough to know the truth."

"No one said you weren't old enough," he said, turning away from me again. "It's just not your time yet."

He fumbled for a few minutes with some things in the bag while I watched the sun burn through the last of the clouds. He handed me a few cracker sandwiches with peanut butter--my favorite--and we sat looking out toward the water. The gulls were conspicuously absent. The only sounds were the crunch of our snacks and the splash of the waves.

By noon the sky was clear and we had an unobstructed view of the still, silent sea. The waves had vanished with the last wisps of fog, off to join the seagulls and the flies in some secret hideaway. No one was in the water. No one else was on the beach. No traffic passed on the road behind us.

My grandfather had been feeding us steadily, as if we would need the energy to face what lie ahead. The heat and the food made me sleepy, and for the first time, with no breeze or other distractions, I could smell the stink and the rot of the shack in which we sat. I tried to shake myself awake. I wanted to walk off the lethargy and breathe in some fresh air, but I felt trapped within the walls surrounding us.

My grandfather had been watching me in my struggle. Now he turned to the water and pointed. I followed his finger with my droopy eyes and saw a bubbling in the waves, about fifty yards off shore. The bubbling grew bigger and moved closer. I could see darkness under and around the displaced water, but it was amorphous in shape and size. My mind would not lock on, would not confirm that it was form and flesh rather than shadow I was seeing. Would not confirm that the dark shape had limbs, or that the large spot of brightness at one end might be an eye, absorbing two tiny humans in its gaze.

My body was as addled as my mind. I sat at the very edge of the blanket, pitched slightly forward. My hands tried uselessly to gain a hold in the sand. Still, their repeated failure was no deterrent to my desperate search for an anchor. My legs were curled under my body, my thighs burning with the extended pose. My back felt straight and brittle, ready to snap at the slightest touch.

As I watched, a deeper darkness appeared in the thing. It was a mouth, opening with a sound of boundless fury. Even from a distance, shielded as I was by a wall of water, it caused the hairs on my body to stand on end, reacting to a call that was monstrous and ancient. The water around the thing rushed into its mouth, creating a thin curtain. I gasped and closed my eyes at the sight of it. When I opened them, the creature was gone.

Within seconds, nature's switch had flipped. A gentle breeze rattled through the walls, bringing the closing cries of gulls and the welcome sound of waves once again slapping against the sand. The stench vanished, replaced by the familiar smells of salt and fish. My body relaxed and I rolled onto my knees, crawled out of the shack, and stood up to stretch and breathe deep and free in the world outside.

It was a dream, I decided. The early fog put me in a dark mood, the food and the heat made me sleepy, delirious, dreaming of a creature that could not be real. I scanned the horizon for anything out of the ordinary and walked a few steps toward the water.

"It was there. It's real," my grandfather said.

I kept my back to him, pretending I couldn't hear. Pretending I hadn't seen what I could not have seen behind that narrow wall of water. I turned around and went back to the shack. I sat down next to my grandfather, took the cheese and summer sausage he offered me, and asked, "Why?"

My grandfather chuckled. "All these generations of men asking 'What' and 'How,' and of course the woman gets to the heart of the matter with 'Why'?"

He sighed and nibbled on a piece of cheese. I ate my own food, waiting for him to answer. In the meantime I turned back to the sea, watching for any signs of the creature. Realizing, finally, why my grandfather sat in the shack every day. Fearing the answers to the questions in my head. Answers I already held inside.

"Truth is, I don't know why. Some sort of curse, I guess. Keeps this family tied to the sea. Destined to live and die by it, no matter what."

"It killed my mother, didn't it?"

My grandfather turned to me, wide-eyed.

"Not directly, I know. But it did, didn't it? Willed her to die, willed something bad to happen so we would come back here?"

He choked on his food and I moved behind him, squatting and thumping on his back. I was trying to save him, and my father, and myself. I was trying to pound out some rhythm of sense from the chaos in my head.

My grandfather nodded and waved to let me know he was okay. I moved back to my spot on the blanket and he turned away from me to sip from his bottle of water.

"Your grandmother drowned trying to save me," he said, still twisted to the side so I couldn't see his face. "And yes, I don't think your mother's cancer was an accident. It happened so fast and she was so young."

He took another sip of water and turned so he was facing forward again. It looked as though someone had moved a slow-motion picture up to speed and I watched him grow a little older as each second passed.

"It wants us here. I think it may even need us here. I think without each other we have no purpose."

He turned to face me. "Does that make any sense?"

It made sense that when I was a child my father tried every night to read me other fairy tales and left in frustration when I insisted on the mermaid tale. It made sense that I had spent my entire life dreaming, imagining another world full of magical, beautiful creatures. I now knew they had been fed to me through a link with a creature that was the abominable truth of the images in my head. It made sense that my father hoped to drown himself in wine and beer long before our family's destiny led him to his fate at the water's edge.

What didn't make sense was my original question. Why? What had happened long ago to satisfy a wicked whim with a family's sacrifice, generation after generation? Was it even a curse? If not, what did we gain from our own destruction? Did it even matter any more? Did it make sense to find a way to stop it? And if I did, was I strong enough to fight destiny?

I sighed heavily and leaned back to rest on my elbows. The life I'd made for myself in my head, my rosy future, flashed before my eyes. It was now as unattainable as the fairy tale, both tainted by the same ugly darkness. I was the first girl born in generations on my father's side. I realized it was my burden to decide the course of my family's legacy.

My grandfather and I looked at each other for a long time without speaking. We were both seeking signs of ourselves in the other, something beyond the same brown eyes and tanned skin. Something under the surface. In him I saw my future; keeping a lonely vigil on a quiet seashore. In me he might have seen his past; the hope dashed when the realization hits you that there is no alternate path for your life.

He broke direct eye contact, glancing at me occasionally as I continued to absorb my fate. I waited until our eyes met again and I nodded. He wept, huge, shuddering sobs that matched the rhythm of the waves eating away at the shore beyond the sanctuary of the shack. I tried to touch him, to hold him, but he kept shifting away from me, like the sand all around us.

* * *

The day my father died was wet and cold. The first rain of the winter had fallen overnight, like an omen. It was barely light outside when the phone rang. I didn't need the caller ID to know it was the hospital. His death was accelerated and inevitable. It was no surprise when the liver went, taking the rest of him with it. Unlike other people around us, I was not surprised how happy he had been to go.

"I never wanted this for you," he told me from his hospital bed the night before, as the first of the raindrops began to fall. "I guess I never fully believed. I thought somehow I could cheat fate instead of accepting it."

"You don't cheat fate," I said. "You accept it or you refuse to believe in it or you fight to change it."

"I changed it, then," he smiled. "I'm free."

It was strange to see my stepmother at my father's funeral. They divorced years before. At the time, she tried to persuade me to follow her to someplace away from my father's drinking and my grandfather's stories. She never knew the full truth, and I ached to tell her now about what drove my father to drink and my grandfather to vigilance and what would eventually claim me as well.

Instead, I told her then that I had to stay to care for them, even if it meant giving up a life of close friends and college parties and finding the path for my future.

We kept in touch, weekly for a while, then monthly, then the requisite "event" updates and holiday letter. Except now there were no events in my life outside of the sea.

"Come stay with me for a while," she pleaded after the service, not even bothering to hide her shock at my gaunt and messy appearance. The words sounded similar to what she'd said years ago.

I began to think, to hope, I could change my fate. My father had gone first, not my grandfather. The natural order of things had been disturbed. Maybe it could continue. Maybe for something so unknown and so unnatural we could negotiate new rules.

I opened my mouth to agree. What could a few days hurt? Then I thought of my grandfather, vulnerable and alone without me. I thought of my grandmother, who died saving him, and my own mother, who died because she was a barrier to fate. I couldn't bear the weight of any more unnecessary grief.

"I'll be okay," I assured her. "This is something I need to work through right here."

I had been getting by on odd jobs that would fill my days but leave my mornings and evenings free to join my grandfather on the beach. We didn't know how much time he had--how much time either of us had--but we spent those precious moments on the sand continuing our old game of painting the colorful details of a magical world below the surface of the water.

The game held no joy for me, now that I knew the truth. Now that I knew there was no fanciful, happily-ever-after world waiting for me. But we played it anyway, as if it was another requirement of our family curse, rubbing wounds raw and swollen, bleeding tears instead of blood. My father had his drinking. We used this as our tool to stave off my disappointment and my grandfather's despair.

* * *

The day my grandfather died was sunny and warm. There was an odd energy in the air, a sense of universal anticipation. It drove me to leave early from my job at the local bookstore and head to the beach. Once again things were calm and muted. As I climbed down the dunes and stood at the corner of the shack I saw my grandfather sitting inside with his eyes closed. His face was slack.

My lips began quivering and tension stabbed across my shoulders as I looked down and realized I was clenching my hands into fists.

I turned to the water.

The bubbles were on the surface, moving closer, growing larger. Now I could see the darkness underneath, until it was no longer an underwater shadow, but a creature emerging from the wet, and towering fifty stories above the beach.

All of the things I thought I had imagined from my first sighting of the creature were magnified to horrific levels. This was no beast born of fairy tale magic, with an ugly exterior and a wise and forgiving heart. This was no cursed being forced to act evilly, with no personal malicious intent. This was a true vision of doom swimming straight out of the deepest dikes of hell.

I felt my grandfather's hand on my arm. I felt myself pulled and falling but I couldn't take my eyes off the creature. I landed hard on my rear in the sand outside the shelter. My grandfather moved forward, toward the water, without looking back.

From my new angle the creature was blocking out the sun. It could not have been less menacing in full light, however. Its skin was a black-brown color and glistening. It reminded me of the leaves around our old house that settled down in wet weather and got lost under bags, only to be rediscovered later, soft and smelling of death.

From its waist down to where its body lay hidden by the water, the creature's skin looked like scales. Other sea animals lived on and among the scales, and strands of seaweed the length of football fields hung limply from various points where it caught on rough patches.

The beast supported itself by leaning on massive hands on the sand. Its arms were the size of a grove of sequoias, and I could only imagine the enormous tail hiding in the waves.

It moved its head to track my grandfather's approach, and I was blinded momentarily by the reappearance of the sun. I didn't feel warm, or cold, or even numb. I had been stricken by an absence of feeling. I tried to stand up, but felt a protective force holding me near the shack.

It was not yet my time to go.

My grandfather continued to walk closer to the creature. As it moved its head slowly from side to side, I felt I was witnessing an ancient ritual, a dance of death I was powerless to stop. The enormous dome continued to undulate on a thick, serpentine neck while I struggled to make out its features.

There were folds of flesh to indicate where ears and a nose might be. The eyes were unmistakable and alarming. Stark white ovals, brighter than lighthouse beacons, anchored by small dark pupils. They never wavered from my grandfather's form, even as the head continued its odd rhythm.

Its mouth was a mere suggestion, a slight protrusion in a line across its smooth face. It was simian and reptilian and nothing known all rolled into one and grown to gargantuan proportions.

My grandfather walked between its massive arms and fully entered its shadow, like a pilgrim approaching his temple. I could no longer see him in the darkness the creature cast and I panicked; I wasn't ready to let him go.

Something new was happening but I couldn't make sense of it. I opened my mouth but no sound escaped. Some part of me realized the creature was opening *its* mouth. For a moment that seemed to last forever, all sound and air and light were pulled into that gaping maw.

The head continued to bob back and forth, mouth open, consuming the energy of life around it. In an instant, the huge jaw unhinged and the head darted forward and down. My grandfather was scooped up in one fluid motion. The head darted back just as quickly. So quickly I wasn't sure at first what had happened, except my grandfather was definitely no longer on the beach.

In that vacuum of time and sound I watched as the creature's jaw moved in slow motion, closing, reattaching to its normal hinged state. And though I knew it was impossible, that it was only the ugliest part of my imagination, I heard the distant, tiny crunch that signaled the end to my grandfather's long and lonely waiting.

The creature ignored me and sank slowly down into the water. As the sea shifted to accommodate its bulk, lids slipped into place over its terrible eyes and it once again became a mysterious shadowy mountain under the waves. A few bubbles marked its final departure, then the water smoothed out before resuming its normal ebb and flow. The sun continued to shine, the wind continued to blow, and the birds continued to circle and drift above, as if nothing had happened.

I was alone.

* * *

There is a shack on the beach made from the bones of the sea. It is a small shelter from the sand and wind, sitting safely above the roar of the waves, nestled in the curve of a ledge bristling with sea grapes.

I have grown old waiting within its walls. I sit stiffly, facing forward, staring out at the sea. I have chosen to break the chain, the curse, the ancient agony that has plagued my family for generations. I am alone in the real world, but here in the shack I am surrounded by happier memories. Here I am straddling two worlds, although I know my time is near to leave both.

In the period immediately following my grandfather's death I craved comfort and companionship. I thought about boarding up the house and running far away to a mountain forest, the frozen north, or the desert, where my link to the water might dry up and blow away like the sand surrounding me. Then I stopped grieving for the life I could have had and faced the truth.

None of us can live without the water. Some of us are simply tied to it more closely than others.

I sit in the shack and listen to my grandfather's voice in my head. I think of the years I sat next to him on that old wool blanket, ignorant of the road that lay ahead. I think of the rare times my father's voice drifted down from the top of dunes, and as I'd scramble out to meet him, the strange excited look of fear in his eyes before he turned his gaze from the water.

I sit and watch that same water, like my grandfather, and many fathers before him. I fear and welcome the day when bubbles appear on the surface, and darkness appears below it. The day when I confront the beast that has infected the blood of my family, shaped our lives, and left us dreaming endlessly of the sea and its secrets.

I have wondered many times over the years if it is adventure and not darkness that has intertwined our paths. Perhaps this end is a new and unimaginable beginning in a world beyond the scope of human understanding. But in the end it doesn't matter the nature of the truth. I have been chosen, and I have chosen to answer the call.

On the day when it is my turn, I hope I will have truly accepted my fate. I tell myself there is no choice, and that I am ready for what awaits me. Yet I am still troubled by the fact that I have decided the destiny for generations that will never be. Once I can make peace with that, I believe my time will be done.

And that will be the day when I am no longer waiting for the fairy tale, when I am living out my own destiny of self-sacrificing love and transcendence. That will be the day when I am brave enough to embrace my chance to forever be free of the sound of pounding waves, and the smell of the salt, and the sight of an ocean of eternal tears.

Green Thumb

It was all over now, surely.

Edward collapsed into the old chair next to the open window and muttered, "What have I done?"

Outside, the few raindrops that had first driven him into the potting shed were now pounding down in a steady stream against the tin roof. He shifted against the disintegrating weave of his seat, the rusting metal frame of the lawn chair grating in protest.

He wanted to sit there like one of those crime drama crooks with his head in his hands until he came up with a clever cover story. But Edward was nothing if not practical. He realized the appeal was more in the romance of that thought and not the reality of it.

Instead, he gripped the crumbly rotting moulding around the window and pulled himself to his feet. He looked outside. Amongst the large, bobbing heads of his roses was a fresh mound of dirt that was becoming increasingly muddy. Soon, Edward feared, the earth would fall away in clumps and uncover, instead of wash away, his sinful deed.

He leaned against the wall to watch, even as water from leaks in the roof began to dampen his hair and drip down behind his spectacles. But the clay proved stronger than him. At long last he had to make a dash from the back of the carefully landscaped yard into the shelter of his cottage home.

"I..I..n-need your h-help," Edward said into the telephone. All those years of therapy and the stutter returned without fail anytime he was under stress.

"With what? Mites? Rust? Honestly, it's raining out, what can you possibly be at?"

"B-bigger p-problem." He huffed several times before continuing. "I've done it. It's all over now. All my hard work for nothing."

He looked down at the pool of dirty water under his green Wellies. Brown tracks led across the otherwise gleaming white tile floor of the kitchen, reminding him of the much bigger mess he had gotten himself into.

"Well? What then?"

Her harsh tone jolted him. His sister had always been the logical one. Stronger, smarter, more successful. Edward, on the other hand, had just managed to eke out an ineffectual existence. Now, in his retirement, he was actually gaining reputation as a champion gardener. Showing himself to be a success and enjoying the attention he was getting for it.

Mostly. Truth be told, he hadn't been fully willing to handle things on his own. All his life he had been told what to do and he did it. That was the practical side of him at work. It just seemed that things went easier that way, didn't it?

Now that he was able to pursue what he wanted, whenever and however he chose, he was frightened by the freedom of it. In fact, he regularly enlisted the aid of his sibling and her knowledge of chemicals to bolster his own efforts in the garden.

And that's what set it off. Set this whole ugly drama in motion. Nosy neighbor Malcolm Bass leaning over the fence where he had no business leaning, asking questions he had no business asking.

* * *

"What you got going there, mate?"

Edward looked up; startled, guilty, gripping the shaker can in his hands.

"Just doing some feeding," he mumbled.

"Must be pretty good stuff, considering all them ribbons you been winning. Which one is that, then?" Malcolm nodded his head toward the can held captive in Edward's hands.

"My own special mixture," said Edward. He went back to sprinkling his plants, making a small show of turning his back to signal the end of the conversation.

"Thing is," said Malcolm, choosing to ignore the hint, "there's rules and such at them competitions about how much one can amend one's plants." He spoke the last few words slowly, enunciating the syllables in an exaggerated fashion.

Edward stood up straight, back still to the fence, feeder can now shaking perceptibly.

"What are you trying to say?" he asked.

"Well, I guess them rules aren't about how much," continued Malcolm, "but by what means exactly."

Edward turned slowly. "Are you accusing me of something?" He bent over with a wracking cough. He had started the day feeling poorly but had wanted to feed his plants before the next storm started, and the skies were growing darker by the minute.

Suddenly Malcolm Bass was at his side, thumping on his back. Despite the assistance, Edward was annoyed his neighbor had hopped the fence on the low end and come to his aid. He grew incensed when Malcolm stopped thumping on his back, picked up the fallen shaker can, and poured out some of its contents into his palm.

"You all right, then?" Malcolm asked absently. He began poking through the granules in his hand, bringing them closer to study at eye level.

"I'm fine," Edward sputtered. "As for your insinuation…"

"Didn't mean nothing by it, old man," said Malcolm as he stopped studying the feed and smiled at Edward. He turned slightly away and made a big show of wiping his palms. "Just making conversation."

Edward wasn't fooled. He saw Malcolm shove some of the formula into a pants pocket before clearing his palms. Edward began trembling. Reaching out to his side, he steadied himself on a nearby shovel handle he'd left upright in the dirt near the site of what would be a new rose bush.

He took a deep, calming breath. He knew there were rules about what you could and could not use on your roses. But there were so many rules, and they changed each year. Edward took another breath. He was sure he hadn't broken any of them.

Well, fairly sure. One thing he was one-hundred-percent sure about was that he could not endure the humiliation of having to return any of the prizes and titles he had won, if by some chance he had inadvertently broken any of those rules. The success made him real, made him something, made him matter. It was the only thing he had.

Malcolm moved toward the fence. "You know me, I like to talk."

Edward froze, certain there was a threat underlying the impish grin and the wink Malcolm tossed over his shoulder. Hadn't Malcolm entered some of those same competitions, shaking his head in wonder as he always came in second or third to Edward? Wasn't he always hanging out with the other neighbors or chatting folks up down at the pub? Who knew what vicious half-truths he was likely to slip into one of those conversations?

Edward debated for a split second then nodded and pulled the shovel free of its resting place. As Malcolm gripped the fence to haul himself back over to his yard, Edward gripped the shovel and swung with all his might.

And so now there was the matter of the muddy mound to deal with.

* * *

"Are you still there?" His sister's voice brought Edward back, her tone warning him she was seconds away from disconnecting the call.

And would that be so horrible, he wondered? Wasn't it his reliance on her that had somewhat gotten him into this thing in the first place?

Enough then. Edward decided he would solve his own problem. He pursed his lips and gave a curt nod that he thought made him seem that much more determined, even if he didn't quite feel it yet. After all, the last time he decided to act on his own thoughts and nodded in agreement with himself, he ended up with a body amongst his rose bushes.

"S-Sorry to have d-disturbed you like this." He fingered a hole in his grey wool jumper. He thought about his roses and his honours and the muddy pile of Malcolm that could bring him down for good. Maybe he shouldn't be so quick to dismiss his sibling's aid. Maybe she could find a chemical solution to his new problem. Or maybe…

Edward smiled and straightened himself up. "Lightning strike had me a bit rattled, it seems," he said.

His voice was louder, clear, confident. "Just had a spot of trouble in the garden, but I'm sure things will look all right once the rain stops."

"Oh. Are you sure?"

"Oh, just so. And thanks for all your help, but I've found a new source of feed for my plants."

"Is that right?"

Edward could tell she was bored and already tuning him out. But he nattered on, triumphant in his newfound freedom and pleased with his practical solution.

"Yes, yes. And I thought maybe I'd buggered the application."

He peered out the back window. The onset of evening and the gloom of the storm made it hard to see, but Edward knew the spot he sought and could picture it in his mind's eye. Meddlesome Malcolm Bass would finally put himself to good use, even if he himself didn't exactly know it.

The irony of the situation was not lost to Edward, and he continued in unconscious relief. "Sometimes these things get so tricky, and you want to be sure you've got it right for the best results. But I think things will work out after all," he said.

As he paused, the dial tone came suddenly. Even his sister's rude impatience didn't faze him. Edward hung up the phone and nodded once again.

"Just a little work to break up the clumps and spread it out evenly," he said as he peered back out the window at his garden. "That's all it will take."

Edward imagined himself sweaty with pickaxe and shovel making substantive, satisfying sounds that meant the end of one problem and the prevention of something similar in the future. This little fright had certainly taught him a lesson. Maybe it even signaled a new path for him to follow. Rid the world of buggers and boost his garden with all-organic ingredients.

Stop. One thing at a time, Edward mused, putting on his practical cap. Focus on the first victory before looking ahead to the next. Because with some hard work and extra care, Edward was certain he would win top prize again this year.

Fear of the Darkness

Christine always viewed herself as a strong, independent woman. She owned and operated an event management company. She bought a condo when she was twenty-five, fixed it up, and rented it out two years later when she and her husband, John, bought their house. She used the overage on the condo rent to supplement their income when John went back to school for his psychology degree. Now, at the age of thirty, Christine was on the fast track to being a millionaire.

She exercised every morning, ate a meticulously balanced diet, and worked in the garden every evening to alleviate the stress of her business. She had three close friends, numerous acquaintances, and a healthy relationship with her parents and older brother. She neither heard nor tracked the movement of her biological clock, and John was in agreement with her on that issue. In fact, they agreed on most things, with one major exception.

Christine was afraid of the dark.

When they were dating, John found it a source of mild amusement. They met for brunch or lunch, daytime sporting events, and movie and theatre matinees. If they went out to dinner or to clubs it was with large groups of people, and he and Christine either left around sunset or stayed out till dawn.

Christine said it was something deep-rooted and primal. She had no interest in discussing it or exploring it; instead, she was willing to work around it and continue on with her life. John, finished with his degree and newly licensed as a therapist, scoffed at her reasoning.

"This is not some sort of 'racial memory' thing, handed down to you from our caveman ancestors. This is not about hiding from some scary beast out there." He leaned in close to her. "It's about hiding from the beasts in here," he said, tapping the side of her head.

Christine pulled away. For a moment, she had a vision of a beast--a tall hairy biped with long claws and fangs, its muzzle dripping with blood, its narrow yellow eyes probing the shadows for movement. She shook her head and the vision vanished. She left the room rubbing her arms as though chilled, but feeling strangely warm inside.

As John's confidence in his profession grew, his prodding did, too. It turned into a daily ritual. At the dinner table, as Christine served dessert, he'd say,

"It's a lovely evening. Should we go for a walk?"

"I'm too tired," she'd answer. "We had a bunch of requests come in today and I'll have to go in early tomorrow and sort them out." Or, "I had a really good workout this morning, so I think I'm just going to rest up for tomorrow." Or, "There's a new book I have that I really want to finish tonight." Or finally, in desperation,

"Why don't we stay in tonight? I'm in an *affectionate* mood."

The weeks went on, the answers continued to rotate; the days grew shorter as they entered autumn. Christine's responses to John's nightly query now noted the chill in the air or the hazard of the sidewalks, slick with wet leaves. His persistence annoyed her, and oddly enough, frightened her. She was unsure of his motives, unsure of why she resisted so strongly, but certain that if she entered the darkness, she would not return.

Halloween loomed. Christine was famous for hosting a large costume party that lasted until dawn. She over-invited people, knowing they'd show up in shifts and fill the gaps left by departing guests. The house was always brightly lit and full of music, games, and food. Trick-or-treaters sailed to the door under a canopy of vibrant orange lights strung through the trees, and votives illuminated the walkway. Christine could look out the window and be comforted by the lack of shadows surrounding her house on this *darkest* night of the year.

"What are you working on?"

Christine jumped. John seemed to be lurking around more these days, watching her, smiling secretively, writing things in a little notebook when he didn't think she could see him. She swiveled around in her desk chair and looked past John to the open office door. She was positive she had closed it earlier, and deliberately hadn't oiled the hinges as she normally would once the weather turned cold and humid. But it hadn't creaked to alert her to John's presence.

"The invitation for the Halloween party," she said, turning and looking up at John, who was staring at the screen behind her.

"Yeah. So, about that. I was thinking maybe we shouldn't do the party thing this year."

Christine swallowed the lump in her throat and fought to control a quavering in her voice. "Why not?"

She continued to stare at him, challenging him to break away from the screen and look her in the eye when he gave whatever excuse he was about to give. Instead, his focus moved up to one of the few bare spots on a wall otherwise filled with bright awards and framed thank you notes from Christine's clients.

"Well, we talked about doing the vacation in Greece in the spring, so we should start saving money for that, make it really first-class, you know?"

Good cover, Christine thought. But she knew the truth of his elaborate explanations, his furtive scribblings, and the tired nightly drama at the dinner table. At least she thought she did, after flipping through his notebook one morning while he was still asleep.

He thought she was crazy.

Possibly paranoid or delusional, he had written. *Suffering from severe achluophobia. Socially dysfunctional.*

She wanted to rip out the pages, wake him up, and stuff the sheaves down his throat until he choked on his arrogance. Instead, she put the notebook back, undamaged. She pretended things were perfectly normal, just as she was pretending now.

"That sounds smart, but we don't have to worry. I just landed a big account that will pay for half of the Greek trip by itself," she lied.

Let him chew on that! She smiled, waiting for his next feint. To her surprise, he lowered his gaze to meet hers.

"Christine, let's just get to the heart of the matter."

He dropped to a squatting position beside her chair, his hands covering hers on the armrest as she twisted to face him.

"You have got to get over this fear of the dark."

"Why?"

"It's not healthy."

"For whom?"

John sighed and stood up, looking once more at the wall.

"For us."

And there it was. The thing Christine truly feared she'd hear if she went on those walks with John at night. The reason they avoided each other's eyes and observed each other like strangers rather than looking, talking, acting like the partners and lovers they were supposed to be.

Bullshit.

She was sounding like John now, examining every little thing for its underlying motives and meaning. It came down to this: she was afraid of the dark, and John was using it as a wedge to drive them apart, when in fact, they had been growing apart ever since he went back to school. Perhaps the divide had begun even earlier, when John's amusement at her plight waned, and he realized he faced a lifetime of "making accommodations" for Christine's extreme fears.

Dammit, she was doing it again!

Christine stood up forcefully, listening to the chair roll across the uneven hardwood floor and clang between the walls in the corner behind her. She watched John; saw him jump away from her and flinch at the collision of metal and plaster, watched his shoulders tense in anticipation of her next move. She felt smug with the power she had over him at this moment. He didn't dare show weakness, didn't dare admit that sometimes you were just afraid of the unknown, *and that was okay.*

Christine had another thought. Maybe John wasn't trying to help her selflessly--out of a sense of duty or the need to alter the functionality of her life. Maybe John was trying to help her because of his own fear. His fear that Christine knew what was *really* out there, waiting in the dark.

She felt nauseous and nervous; her hands had gone clammy. She took a deep breath. For a moment, she felt a thousand times stronger than she had mere moments before. She was tempted to explore this feeling, to find out why and how she could feel these conflicting sensations. But John spoke.

"I think we really need this time alone, Christine."

He looked at her in a way she had nearly forgotten. She was ready to go to him and let him hold her and comfort her and perform whatever head-shrinking voodoo was necessary to make him look at her like that again, all of the time.

"I think we can work together to get you to some sort of breakthrough."

Just as suddenly, the magic vanished. Christine felt the familiar wave of nausea and the prickling of goose bumps on her arms. At the same time, somewhere deep inside and fighting its way rapidly to the surface was the realization she didn't need John's help.

Or anyone else's for that matter.

It was all a trap. She saw that now. John would keep her here alone on Halloween and he'd turn out the lights and he'd try to reassure her everything would be all right, that she would be all right, he wouldn't let anything or anyone hurt her. His intentions might be good; he might believe what he was thinking. Yet Christine knew, with every fiber of her being, that when the lights went out, there was no going back. The hurt would be indescribable, and the darkness would win.

John, looking concerned about her silence and the conflicting emotions battling for control of her face, moved closer. Christine stiffened, but allowed him to hold her, to become complacent; secure in the power of what he thought he knew. It was some sort of destiny she was fighting, Christine realized, and it was going to end with her death. The moment she admitted that to herself, she found peace.

The days ticked by and Christine forged ahead with renewed energy. She wrapped up lingering accounts, delegated the work for new accounts, and secretly got her legal affairs in order. With her garden mostly dormant, she raked leaves and tried new gourmet recipes to fill her late afternoon time. She met her friends for lunch, her mother for high tea, her father for a round of golf, and her brother for a day of playing "hooky" shopping at the mall--eating junk food, and sneaking into movies like they'd done when they were teenagers.

On the night of October 30 she sprinkled red roses in a path from the front door to the bedroom, where she waited for John in a barely-there negligee with a bottle of chilled champagne and a large tub of whipped cream. Despite her misgivings about his plan, she intended to leave this world with no regrets.

Halloween morning. Christine awoke with the now-familiar sensations of nausea, chills, and underlying strength. She had ruled out pregnancy several days before with a home test. At least she wouldn't be taking an innocent life with her.

She took the day off from work, cleaned the house, studiously avoided the pantry cupboard that held the candy for the evening's trick-or-treaters, and went through her files one last time to make sure everything was in order. In her organizing she found a journal. It was so old she didn't even remember having it, until she opened to a page and saw the sprawling handwriting she used as a junior high student. There were entries about boys and her friends and school, and scattered here and there were references to a recurring nightmare.

Christine flipped back to the beginning of the book until she found the first entry on the nightmare. Her younger self described a complicated feeling of dread mixed with elation, much like what Christine had been feeling these past few weeks. Then she went on to detail the same creature that had appeared in Christine's daydream months ago.

This is how I will die, eleven--year-old Christine had written after the description of the beast.

This is how I will die.

* * *

John came home early for dinner so their meal wouldn't be interrupted by the doorbell. Somehow he convinced Christine to forgo the lights and the candles outside. When she opened the door to the first eager faces, she was shocked at how small and vulnerable they appeared, lit only by the yellow porch light.

Every half hour, John went to another room in the house and turned off the lights. Christine tried to stifle her anxiety by focusing on the painted faces and costumes appearing in a steady stream at the door, but by ten o'clock, the sounds of childish laughter and the ring of the doorbell were memories. John turned off the outside light while Christine sat on a large pillow in the living room in front of the fireplace, absently nibbling on the last of the candy. John sat beside her and they stared silently into the fire.

"Are you ready?"

Eleven o'clock. Christine's head moved, almost imperceptibly. John crossed the living room and flipped the last light switch. He moved quickly back to

Christine's side and brushed away the tears blanketing her cheeks.

"You've been very brave."

Christine sighed, but said nothing.

"I'm very proud of you for facing your fear like this."

John hugged Christine and she hugged back. She wished he'd pull some sort of adolescent prank, some act to scare her so he could turn on the lights to show how silly she had been. She would rather end the night angry with him than have the night never end. Instead, they cuddled in front of the fire and Christine could feel herself growing sleepy. She leaned her head against John's shoulder and closed her eyes.

She wasn't sure how much time passed before she heard it—the low, long growl of a large animal. Her eyes flew open. The sound was nearby, and the light from the fire was nearly out, leaving the room in massive shadow.

"What was that?!" John shot up onto his knees and looked around.

Without John's arms to support her, Christine flopped to one side. She could feel her heartbeat slowing. Her lungs were surrendering their air. Her eyelids fluttered then snapped close, placing her in utter darkness.

"It's my destiny," she mumbled before passing out.

* * *

She was dying.

Christine knew this, standing in front of the sink in the half bathroom. The house was cold and dark and quiet. The only light came from the moon through the bathroom window. She stared at herself in the mirror. She was covered in blood, unrecognizable, and with each second she felt the last of her life energy draining away. She slumped to her knees and rested her forehead against the cool base of the sink. Dark smears traced the features of her face across the white porcelain.

Her final thought was of John. He had been right all along about the beast dwelling within.

* * *

The creature stood up and exited the bathroom. It clomped across the floor on heavy feet, passing John's mangled corpse, which lay in front of the fireplace. A drop of blood fell from the fur on its face, and its long tongue lashed out to rescue the precious liquid before it could hit the floor. No capacity for regret or remorse. No thoughts, no memory of the host being whose human shell had finally cracked enough to bring the beast forth.

Destiny.

The creature wrestled with the front door before tearing it, deadbolt and all, off the hinges. It sniffed the night air, full of fear, mischief, and evil. It scoped the shadows with golden eyes, glittering with the promise of prey.

Then it stepped out into the darkness, ready to begin its new life.

Fountain of Youth

As he lowers me into the chamber, I panic. Am I doing the right thing?

He can't miss my clenched hands, curled toes, shoulders tightened into a shrug even though I'm lying flat on my back. The sensory suit is supposed to insulate me from the influences of the outside world, but I feel chilled as I leave the bright lights and relative warmth of the laboratory, and fall deeper into the darkness of the deprivation cubicle.

Dr. Channing uses his calming voice, his precise clipped words forming a beat on which I can focus. My hands unclench but the rest of me is tense and unyielding. I can't see him, but in my head I can picture him on the other side of the laboratory window, bending his tall, lean frame over to watch a bank of monitors that measure my physical and mental state.

He speaks slowly into the headset microphone he uses during our weekly sessions. He says the auto recording allows him to focus his attention on me instead of having to take notes. Here in the lab, his VR visor will be lying off to the side while he waits for when I am completely under. Then, he says, he can observe what happens when I return to the past and face my demon.

I wasn't sold on the idea at first, not at all. The idea of someone entering my darkest hour and watching what happened to me, seeing my fear and pain and helplessness--it felt like I would be violated all over again. There was nothing he would be able to do. No aid he could give while I was under. It seemed pointless, then, to have someone else frustrated by the same, unchanging sequence of events. I described it to him as humiliation squared. But somehow Dr. Channing made it all make sense.

From the beginning, it seemed he understood what I had gone through. I worked part-time in a counseling center, ironically and consciously avoiding the baggage left by my childhood molestation. Dr. Channing was a guest speaker at our annual fundraising event, an expert in regressive therapy whose talk sounded good but whose methods I doubted till I got to know him better during the event's gala dinner.

Normally careful about what I revealed to strangers, I found myself opening up as soon as Dr. Channing asked how I had come to work at the center. He had an empathetic air about him. He validated my lack of trust; why I pushed men away or exacted revenge on the stubborn ones who tried to stick around. He suggested private sessions and, though I was reluctant to try therapy, especially with a male therapist, he made the offer impossible to resist.

For years Dr. Channing had been working on an experimental therapy--a state of deep hypnosis where someone could return to a particular day, a particular incident, and change the outcome in his or her mind. To say that it was controversial was an understatement. But he argued that the human mind frequently took measures to protect itself following trauma, and with his therapy the survivor would feel empowered rather than confused or betrayed. My weekly therapy sessions with Dr. Channing were free of charge as a prelude to me trying his memory-altering approach.

"If you have the chance, why not regain your youth? Your life?" he had asked me.

"I don't think I'm ready," I countered. At the time we were only a few months into therapy, and though I felt I was making some progress, I didn't feel strong enough to relive that nightmare and bring an observer along in the bargain. Twenty years of agony cannot be conquered in just three months.

Eventually he brought it up again. We were many more months into our sessions and I was feeling more in control, more sure of who I was and who I wanted to be. Despite the idea's continued lack of support among his colleagues, I felt a growing sense of hope when Dr. Channing talked about his new therapy. I saw it as an opportunity to help myself and others. I was finally ready to wake up from my lifelong nightmare.

So now I find myself here, still a bit unsure, but more willing to try. I close my eyes and listen, and let go. I'm floating out of time, but I don't fear my freedom. I take a deep breath and let it out slowly. I concentrate on the weight of my tongue as the air whistles through my teeth. I exhale and hear the first noises in my mind, muted, as though broadcast from behind a closed door.

I breathe in. The door opens.

I breathe out. I am no longer aware of Dr. Channing's voice.

I open my eyes, and I'm back.

Leavenworth, Kansas. Spring 1982.

The sun is strong and I blink against its brightness. I feel the warmth rising from the blacktop as I watch boys and girls play tetherball and swing on the swings and run screaming in and around the teachers, playing tag. I smile at the sound, the pure joy around me. I feel the urge to run, to jump, to climb with my friends. But I turn away from the laughter and safety, and face the field that spreads out forever behind the school grounds.

I know what I must do.

The path is hidden. I first found it by accident, now find it by muscle memory, and marvel at the size of the sunflowers filling the field. The tops of the flowers bob around in the breeze, but they always seem to keep their brown faces looking down at me.

After a while I realize I can only hear the rustle of the plants around me. I turn around, but the path that has led me this far has vanished. I can't see the school or the teachers or the scampering children. I rub my arms, focusing on their sunbaked warmth. I take another deep, sweet breath and turn around again.

Should I stop here and surrender to the cheery mass encircling me? I wonder how the sunflowers will feel against my face--smooth and velvety, or rough like the tongue of a cat? Ahead of me, I can see them begin to drop over the edge of the horizon. They mark the path I must take, and I marvel that they have always been my favorite flower.

I move slowly forward.

Now I'm standing on the edge, with everything just as I remember it. The wind has died, and the sunflowers have stopped shifting. The sun feels hotter without the breeze, and sweat is trickling down my nose and the back of my neck. Somewhere behind me, someone is calling my name. But she won't find me, not yet. Not before he finds me again.

I look down. At the bottom of the hill is a narrow dirt road. In my childhood memory the hill is steep and long, like a cliff dropping down to another place far below. But now I can see it's just a hill, just a handful of long strides for an adult to traverse.

On the side of the road is a dusty car. All of these years, all of my life, and the rhyme comes back into my head:

A. B. C. Brown. Florida Datsun. 1.2.3.

The car door opens and a man gets out. He shields his eyes against the sun and looks up at me. His face is in shadow because of his large hand, but I can see that he's smiling.

"Such a pretty little thing," he says, in a slow, deep drawl. He's holding a baby doll in his free hand, and she's wearing a shiny blue dress. I know, though, that he's talking about me and not the baby doll. He holds her up for me to see.

"Why don't you come on down here and talk to me?"

He's already moving in my direction, impossibly fast up the hill and closing the distance between us while I stand frozen. In my eyes he is a mile high and his hands seem eager to grab hold of something, since he has tossed the doll aside. Something inside me clicks and I turn and run, crashing wildly through the sunflowers, bending stems until their heavy heads are colliding with the ground in my wake.

I try to remember what I wanted to do here, why I came back, but my fear has pushed everything out of my head. I hear the man coming through the sunflowers behind me, grunting and gaining ground, and I am an animal looking only for a way to escape.

Suddenly, there's a shadow on my left. I pause, and it moves in front of me and blocks my way. None of this is right. None of this is how it happened the first time. And then I remember that's why I'm here--to change things--but this is not the way I wanted it to go.

It was supposed to start like it did the first time, when I went down the hill, just for a minute, just to see the beautiful doll he held in his hands. I could hear the recess teacher calling my name then, but I didn't care. It was just going to be for a minute.

But in that minute he grabbed me, with one big hand covering my mouth, smelling of gasoline and cigarettes, and the other slipping down into my shorts, his fingers scrabbling into my secret places with a very lonely anger.

This time I was going to stop him before it could happen. To fight back, to call to the teacher, something. Now I was the one who was angry and lonely and determined to be in control. Instead, he is here where he is not supposed to be and I am caught off guard as he towers over me with his hands on his hips.

He pushes a sunflower aside and the sun strikes his face. I scream, and the door in my mind closes.

* * *

"I don't understand why I can't control it," I said. We were in Dr. Channing's office after yet another session where the details of the encounter had changed but I was still unable to effect the change *I* wanted. Where were all of these variables coming from?

"It is puzzling," he mused. "You seem to be ready to address this, and yet…"

"And yet what?"

"Perhaps your focus on trying to control every aspect of the situation is causing a split."

"What do you mean?"

"With so many possible variables it could be that your mind is running through ones that seem most plausible for you," explained Dr. Channing.

"On a subconscious level, of course," he added, in response to my skeptical pout.

"So what should I do?"

"Focus on one thing you want to change," he said. "One thing at a time instead of multiple things at once. Your mind needs time to readjust and build your new story of what happened."

I nod. I think for a while, and come up with one small thing I want to change. I tell Dr. Channing about it and he seems pleased.

I don't tell him about the other thing. I want to test it. Most of the criticism of Dr. Channing's method comes from the fallout of the regressive therapy and hypnosis techniques I heard about in my youth. The false memory issue where patients "remembered" abuse that may have never happened. I have the opposite problem--I know the abuse happened, but don't particularly want to remember the ugly and vulnerable details every minute of my life.

Dr. Channing's colleagues write that his therapy is nothing more than actively planting false memories, and there's no guarantee that a patient so willing to subvert the truth wouldn't later have problems distinguishing reality in other parts of their lives.

They all make the mind sound like a buffet, where anyone can walk up and pick and choose what they want, and someone will take away the unpopular options and replace them with something more appetizing. The problem is in real life, at the end of the day, there's no one to clean things up and shut down to get ready for the next day.

Except me.

I need to know that it's really, truly me in control of my destiny.

* * *

As he lowers me into the chamber, I panic. Am I doing the right thing?

He can't miss my clenched hands, curled toes, shoulders tightened into a shrug even though I'm lying flat on my back. He speaks, and my hands and toes relax, but my shoulders are still tense in anticipation of what may be.

I breathe deeply, thinking of the small thing I want to change and the bigger thing I want to try.

My decisions, my power, my life, I repeat to myself. The door in my mind opens.

I feel the warmth of the sun, hear the noise of the playground, see the sunflowers bobbing in the field. I make my way to that familiar place where the car is waiting and he is there and I am surprised but not surprised to see the color of the doll's dress is now a bright yellow to match the sunflowers.

I hear the teacher's voice behind me but I do not hesitate. I continue down the hill, to meet him where it first happened, and not in the sanctuary of my sunflowers.

He has started toward me but stops as I keep moving forward. I look past him to the car, the brown Datsun.

"Your car has a Florida license plate, but we're in Kansas," I say with the direct and indistinct logic of a fifth grader.

He freezes for a moment then drops the doll and grabs my arm. Behind me the teacher's voice grows louder and I look over my shoulder to see her worried face at the top of the hill.

I look back and the man is unconcerned as he pulls me close to him. The sunlight bathes his face and I see his smile and I scream and the door in my mind closes.

* * *

"I needed to know," I said.

Dr. Channing is not pleased with me. I can feel waves of his disapproval, almost like they are a tangible thing, chastising me as if I were a child who has disappointed her parent.

Before, I might have defended my actions, but I remind myself I should give no apologies for doing what's right for me. It is my mind and my memories and my decisions on how I can move forward. Still, I am nervous about the palpable tension and his reaction.

Have I done myself harm that I cannot see? Turned back time on progress we have made?

He says nothing to either of these points. In fact, he says nothing, breathing deeply as he looks at a spot over my head. I realize he's trying to gain control once again.

"This won't work if you don't trust me," he says.

He has taken a deep breath and his jaw is unclenched but I can see the tension in his shoulders as he drops his gaze down to me. "We are partners in this effort, right? And partners need to share and rely on each other."

I nod and look away. For the first time in our association I am uncomfortable. I feign remorse, but I don't know why I feel the need to cover my own true feelings. His reaction seems outsized and inappropriate, and I wonder why it matters so much to him. Surely his professional reputation is not more important than the future of my mental health?

* * *

As he lowers me into the chamber, I panic. Am I doing the right thing?

He can't miss my clenched hands, curled toes, shoulders tightened into a shrug even though I'm lying flat on my back. He speaks, and my hands and toes relax, but my shoulders are still tense in anticipation.

I walk through the same playground, the same sunflower field. I reach the same edge of my small world and run from my attacker, only to have him block me from the path to safety. His face is shadowed but there's something tugging at me, something I need to remember to make this different than it was before.

"So much sweeter the next time around," he murmurs.

He bends down and I'm screaming now, because I can see and I remember. Those eyes, the same flat brown eyes that have watched me in my weekly sessions as I poured out the details of my ruined life. In this face--his *real* face, they are so cold that I have forgotten about the sun and the flowers and I am trapped in a raw and bitter darkness.

He turns at the sound of the teacher calling my name. She has heard me scream, and I can trace her progress through the field as flower heads sway and nod and stalks crack in the wake of her rapid passage.

The first time, the teacher found me on the side of the road, rumpled, crying, bleeding, and choking in the dust of the car that sped away at her approach. I couldn't tell her what happened, just kept repeating my little rhyme until they figured out it was the car and license plate of my attacker. But they never found him.

I breathe deeply, and remind myself why I'm here. Remind myself of the wasted life that I'm living, the life I want to reclaim from the one who took it away in the first place.

I assume a fighting stance. He laughs. I channel my anger and frustration and fear, my martial arts training at the gym, and lash out at him with my future in the balance.

And miss.

I've forgotten about my nine-year-old limbs; shorter, smaller, less coordinated than I would like them to be. He laughs again. He licks his lips and moves closer.

"You don't understand, do you?" he says. His speech is no longer slow and husky. Now he speaks like the Dr. Channing he has become, and I feel tears forming as I shake my head at the deception--the one he has created and the one created by my mind.

"This trip was never for *you* at all. You are *my* fountain of youth. Through you I can go back to a time when I was young and strong and powerful. I can relive my greatest moments or I can change the details and find new ways to play inside your head. And then I can make you forget everything and we can do it all over again, just like the last time, and the time before that, and--"

The teacher breaks through the flowers into the spot where we are standing, and I feel a surge of hope. But before she can speak he moves quickly to her, placing one hand over her mouth and using the other to remove the knife from his back pocket, flip open its blade, and stab her through the heart.

He drops her body to the ground and turns back to me. He is speaking, but the words are like the renewed breeze through the sunflowers, just a chilly dull rustle in the background. I stare at the woman at his feet, looking very much like a larger version of the doll he had held in his hands. I want very much for her to be alive, to speak, to move, to help me.

I glance up. He's still talking, looking at me, but through me. I look again at the body on the ground. A finger twitches. Her palm slowly curls in upon itself. She has rolled her head to look at me. I could will her to get up, to take the knife from her chest and finish him off, but I stop myself. I move my eyes away so he can't see where I'm looking.

I remember somehow, sometime, thinking this before. About taking the knife and stopping him for good. I haven't because I wasn't ready to accept everything he has done to me, but I knew somewhere inside that each time I come back here I grow stronger. And he doesn't know--he can't know anything more than what I let him see. So once again, I raise my blank face to him.

"Let's try this again." He smiles down at me.

I hear the trigger word from somewhere far away, and when I come back to myself I am sweaty and trembling on the table in the lab. The taste in my mouth is dust and dirt, and there are tears on my face.

I feel an overwhelming sense of urgency; there is something important for me to remember. A broken doll, empty eyes, a flash of silver and red, an unnatural cold. But when I sit up, the feeling is falling away in pieces that I struggle to gather and reassemble.

* * *

As he lowers me into the chamber, I panic. Am I doing the right thing?

He can't miss my clenched hands—

I look down at them, watching my fingers curl out and then back in toward my palms. They are strong, but there is another set of hands I remember. Also strong. But angry. Evil. And they must be stopped.

I remember it all and grimace. I glance to where he waits to rip my world open once again.

But not today. It's time to play the part. I make my face look anxious. I scrunch my shoulders into a shrug. I curl my toes and tighten my fists.

I'm finally ready for the last round of this fight.

The Back Seat

She looked down at her hands where they gripped the steering wheel. Tensely, tightly, clinging so hard that the veins stood out like bluish-green strings under her skin.

No, not strings, she thought. Bands. Stretched to the limit and waiting to snap, which would leave her hands hanging limp and useless from the ends of her arms. Right now it all held together in some delicate balance of form and function. But there was something about her hands that set her teeth on edge.

She could feel those islands of enamel in her mouth, also gripping tightly. Incisors, bicuspids, molars pressing against each other in an attempt to merge. She glanced at herself in the rearview mirror, waiting for a grind, a crack, a shift to ease the ache in her jaws.

She focused again on her hands. There was something hideous about them. Not at first sight, although they looked so tiny with the fingers hiding on the other side of the wheel. Like they were truncated, miniature Muppet hands at play. There was something bad about them she couldn't quite see, but she knew it was there. Waiting, taut and terrible under the surface of her skin. Just like her bluish-green rubber-band veins.

A horn sounded. Then again. And again. Each instance had an exponential effect, bouncing and echoing around in the tunnel. The blaring swelled until she thought she could actually see the sound polluting the air. She wanted to cover her ears, but her hands were glued to the wheel.

The noise crowded out her thoughts and filled her senses until she could hear-touch-taste-smell nothing but the blat caused by hand to horn. She felt nauseous and congested and hoped the pain traveling from her jaw to her temple signaled that it would soon be over. Then she wouldn't have to live with what she knew and felt but couldn't seem to remember. Something about what her hideous hands had done.

Suddenly the sound stopped and the tunnel was quiet. And dark. Only a few cars ever obeyed the daytime headlights sign in the tunnel. She was not one of them, and apparently neither were any of her fellow travelers. She tried, but her hands wouldn't move to flick them on. In the feeble trickle of daylight, however, she could see no movement. After the cacophony of horns, the stillness was unsettling.

Then she thought she heard an echoing thud. Car doors slamming shut in anger, frustration, fear? But no one walked past her car, in front of her car, behind her car. She checked all of her mirrors. No shifting shadows, no shapes peering in windows or trying to make contact.

Hands still gripping the wheel, she turned from side to side. No one. No one outside their car, anxiously pacing the lanes. No one climbing the curb to the emergency phone to report the broken lights. No eerie display of backlit screens as people grappled with cell phones to call about traffic, notify babysitters, or solicit comfort from loved ones. No one sat inside their cars, nor on top of their cars. No one stood or paced or raged at the inexplicable delay.

There was no one else in the tunnel.

In the silence she continued to sit upright in her seat, hands on the wheel, eyes facing forward. She knew the radio was broken. She knew the glove box was empty. She had no cell phone. She thought she might have a purse, tossed carelessly in the back seat. Perhaps she could find something in there to distract her from whatever it was that was trying to creep into the near-memory corners of her mind. But she could not bring herself to turn around.

She no longer willed her hands away from the wheel. Instead, she was happy to see them rooted there, safe. They were not busy doing bad things. Besides, the car smelled of stale smoke, sweat, and something else. She was sure the something-else smell was coming from the back seat.

She wanted to wake up. She had to be dreaming. Caught up in some slowly building nightmare she didn't want to see through to the end. She didn't know this place, did she? Not like this. Not with dripping walls and daytime darkness. She was confused, and incredibly tired. She couldn't remember where she had come from or where she was going. Why she wasn't moving. Or why she was alone.

She tried again to focus but her thoughts were fuzzy and disjointed. Her hands reacted with their own will, spasm after spasm, jerking to try to turn the key and kill the ignition.

She shuddered. No, not kill. She didn't like that word. Stop. Soften. Quiet. Yes...quiet.

Her hands failed in their mission and flopped back to rest on the lower part of the steering wheel. She sat in the darkness with only the rumble of her idling engine accompanying her and the doors locked and the windows up tight. Somehow that seemed wrong and right at the same time, everything okay except for that back-seat-something smell, nagging and poking and prodding at her thoughts.

A small seed of fear appeared somewhere deep inside, took root, and bloomed. She could feel tendrils tickling out along her limbs, pushing up the hairs on her arms. Dark petals forced their way into her throat, suffocating her. She coughed and gagged. Her hands would not obey her command to move and claw at what caught in her throat. She would die here, senselessly sitting alone in this dark endless tunnel.

(Alone? Not alone. The back seat! The back—)

Now her entire body tickled. It was that unpleasant sensation just before a cough, when the muscles in your throat tighten and your eyes water. Or when you feel the urgent need to scratch at something when there's nothing there. Or, when looking down, you see a multi-legged creature crawling across your skin.

Panicking now, she rocked her head from side to side, forward and backward, trying to shake out the sensation. She focused her attention outward, visualizing what she wanted to do, willing her body to perform. She struggled again for the key, one hand batting at it uselessly, causing it to swing back and forth like a hypnotic pendulum.

The tickle had traveled up behind her eyes and she blinked rapidly with no effect. She was going to lose this fight, she thought. She focused on her hands again, mentally flexing each finger. She begged and pleaded for one of them to obey her. They wanted her to stay and suffer. To pay for how she had used them to do bad things.

Screaming.

She could hear it, but it was so far away, like it was coming from the other side of the tunnel. It got louder, came closer, was all around her until she remembered how she had felt such fear and anger and overwhelming disappointment.

Screaming. Baby doll screaming. From the back seat, and the high chair, and the bathtub, and the bassinet. Ceaseless, mindless, cruel caterwauling.

Bad baby doll.

Everyone knew babies were supposed to sit there and look cute in their frilly dresses and shiny shoes and dimpled skin and brushable hair, and giggle and smile and pout and maybe cry a little, but not scream. Not that. That was too much.

She wanted to send it back. Anyone would agree it was defective. She demanded perfection, and this doll was flawed and needed to be returned. He wouldn't let her. He laughed and patted her head and said she'd feel better soon. She'd be back to her old self and she'd see just how much it was a precious present they were lucky to have for their very own.

She endured, she indulged and the screaming stopped but the baby got bigger and the demands got broader and the tantrums got louder and her patience got shorter.

Mama. Mama. Mama.

She tried and she pleaded and she dreaded every day for an eternity, it seemed. And he smiled and said things would keep getting better, and then he would leave her alone with the doll-demon for the day. Every day.

Mama! Mama! Mama!

She told him she'd had enough and that he had to take the doll away and get her another one. He had stopped smiling and nodding with patient understanding. Now he scowled and swore and told her it was her problem to fix.

As a child she had always loved her dolls. She dressed them and talked to them and took them to tea. If they were ugly she made them pretty with makeup or new clothes or new hair. When they got broken or dirty or boring she'd get rid of them and get new ones to love. But if he wouldn't let her get a new one, she'd have to be practical.

She thought for a while about different ways to repair things that didn't work the way they were supposed to work. No job for tape or glue, though. And no way she could see to tighten up anything that might be loose. So maybe something was too tight and actually needed loosening. Maybe after some fixing, things would work the way they were supposed to.

Sure enough, with a little jiggle (or two, or three--she couldn't remember exactly), she had fixed that doll right up. After the adjustment, it sat quietly while she dressed it in a brand new outfit and put a lovely bow in its fine baby-doll hair. But now it was always watching her like in one of those scary movies. Even though she had fixed its screaming, it still seemed to be broken.

Was that why she was in the tunnel? To take back the doll? To give it away to someone else? It must be in the back seat. Maybe if she looked at it she'd remember. But she didn't want to. Not really. Each time she started to turn around and take a peek, she stopped herself. When she noticed a noise coming from outside her car, she was relieved.

Beeping. Somewhere in the depths of the tunnel in front of her. It was familiar, but she couldn't remember why.

Red light blinking danger.

She was entering a soft, sweet, twilight of terror but she couldn't put the pieces together enough to do something about it. Red. Stoplight? But she had to go.

To keep going even though she was so sleepy now and it seemed she would never get out of this tunnel.

And she remembered now, how he had opened the small door into the tunnel and called out to her. (No, that couldn't be right, could it? How did he get to the tunnel? *Her* tunnel?) He came to her and then he looked in the back seat and saw the silent, no-longer-misbehaving doll and cried out and was suddenly very angry.

He grabbed her and pulled her out of the car and was shaking her just like she had shaken the screaming baby doll. And it hurt. She was surprised by how much it hurt to be adjusted. He dragged her to the back seat and pointed and yelled but she wouldn't look, he couldn't make her, and she kicked him and backed away. Then those hands, those practical doll-adjusting hands grabbed something from the wall of the tunnel (no, that definitely couldn't be, could it?) and hit him again and again till he fell over, into the back seat, down on the floor, safe and still under the creepy stare of the soundless doll.

She remembered now, closing the large door of the garage--no, tunnel--and turning on the car. The wheels might not move, but she would still get away. No more screaming. No more shaking. No more yelling. No more.

So here she was, sitting and sleepily waiting. She had never been so patient. Let the walls drip and the something-stench try to reach her from the back seat. She was calm now, smiling dreamily. Something was happening. She could feel it as her misunderstood hands dropped softly from the wheel to rest in her lap.

She could no longer hear the detector beeping. She no longer minded the darkness. She embraced the silence. She knew her trip was finally coming to an end. And she would never have to look in the back seat.

Renasci

How art thou fallen from heaven, O Lucifer, son of the morning!
--Isaiah 14:12

The baby was in the middle of the road.

At first it sat upright, its chubby, milky arms spinning in small circles to hold its balance. Its head seemed overly large--bald and bulbous like a human shallot. Eventually its arms stopped moving and it seemed to fall in on itself, the occasional upheaval of breathing the only outward sign of life.

Maria stopped staring at the baby and looked around. There were no cars, no other pedestrians, no one else in sight. The night was hot and humid. Mosquitoes and other flying annoyances gathered in large, tight balls under the hooded streetlights, like buzzing topiaries.

The street was narrow, hemmed in by wide sidewalks bordering identical houses with darkened windows. Each yard was perfectly square, perfectly clipped, with grass so green it seemed to glow brightly, even in the shadowed light.

This was a far cry from the urban brownstone neighborhood Maria called home. Her street was wide and busy. The sidewalks were home to dying trees sprouting from broken concrete, and strewn with plastic bags and food litter, broken toys, and feces of unknown origin. The steps leading up or down to each residence were usually lined with young children, seniors, and the unemployed. It was loud and smelly and Maria loved it.

The houses lining *this* street were more than dark; they were empty, sterile. There was no sense that someone cared for them or that together they formed a real community. Maria remembered a vacation she took, eons ago, when she visited a movie set that looked just like this street. The everyday place that had never existed.

She glanced again in the baby's direction, confirming that it still sagged motionless in the road. She felt fear, but not for the baby's safety. She felt fascination, but was also repulsed. She wanted to move away from the baby and from this place, but she needed to know what was happening, try to remember what had already happened, and perhaps figure out what might happen next.

Maria looked down. She was barefoot, in denim cutoff shorts and a white cotton tank top. The clothes were unfamiliar. This morning she left home in a long-sleeved blouse, long skirt, and sandals. She was walking the five blocks to work when she first saw him—it—she couldn't remember which was right, but something told her it was both. She couldn't remember what happened after that.

Now Maria was willing herself to touch the strange clothes she wore, to probe pockets or folds for clues.

Those arms. The legs below them. So pale that they harbored blue shadows. They were utterly unfamiliar, and Maria realized that this body was not her own.

Her own body was petite, with smooth brown skin across taut muscles. That was the body that had begun the walk to work this morning in flowy peasant clothes. This body, this shape she now wore, was oversized, awkward, and flabby, like the baby-sitting in the middle of the road.

The baby sat up again.

As she watched him, Maria felt something. She looked down. A toe moved. Then another. Soon all ten toes wriggled and Maria could feel the warm asphalt under her feet. Against her will, she took tentative steps toward the child. Stones and bits of glass worked their way under the curves of her toes and slid along the soles of her feet, but there was no pain.

The baby rolled to its knees. No longer an alabaster bundle of diapered flesh, it wobbled slowly onto tiny legs and, after a few shaky steps, walked steadily toward the darker end of the street.

There was a park there, with playground equipment caught in halos from the few working streetlights. Maria pictured herself pushing the baby in a swing, higher and higher until the rusted chains wrapped around the upper bar of the swing set and snapped, hurling the baby out onto the grass with a thump.

Or perhaps the two of them would twirl together on the creaky red merry-go-round, spinning faster and faster until Maria had to let go of the baby to hold on for herself. She would watch the baby's eyes and mouth open wide, but the cry would be cut off as the tiny body shot out into space, beyond the limits of Maria's dizzied vision.

The thoughts made her of two minds. She was happy at the thought of being free of the baby. Of watching a moment of joy turn to terror in payment for something that had been or would be done to her. She was also sick with shame. How could a woman, a mother, think such horrible thoughts about a defenseless child?

Some part of Maria wanted to save the baby, to chase down its future tormentors, impale them with their instruments of menace, and protect the child from harm. She would walk through fire for it, nurture and feed its every dark desire, willingly sacrifice everything. It was this part that controlled her limbs and compelled her to struggle forward.

The rest of her, the Maria part of her, wanted to run. The real her didn't have a baby. Hadn't wanted a baby the one and only time she'd been pregnant. That part of her somehow knew that to stay in this place, to embrace that child, was to suffer and die and suffer again.

The baby was moving too fast. Maria's legs were still asleep, stumping along on feet that had barely tingled into awareness, while her arms uselessly tried to pump her numb body forward. She was only halfway down the block when the baby disappeared completely into the shadows.

Maria stopped. The effort to move had caused her to sweat. Her hair was damp, sending streams of saline down her neck and along her cheeks. A stinging drop fell into one eye and she slowly shook her head to clear her sight.

She no longer saw the park or the suburban ghost town surrounding her. She was back at home, in her own body, performing on stage. As always, she turned herself inward, reaching for the joy or the fear or the sadness she needed to convey to the audience through her movements.

A commotion in the front row drew Maria out, bringing her into eye contact with a woman in the first row that had gone into labor. The performance halted, the rhythm of the auditorium now dictated by the woman's cries, alternating with her desperate panting. Then the woman's eyes rolled up into her head and she flopped to one side as the baby slipped out between her legs and silently took its place in the world.

That was the body Maria now inhabited, she realized. The body of the baby's mother, pasty and stiff because it was no longer living. How had she come to be here, trapped in this corpse, an unwilling and unfeeling guardian of a day-old baby that, mere moments ago, had stood up and walked away?

There was another noise in the night. A rustling of leaves from the park at the end of the street. The insects stopped buzzing and moved away. Maria felt warm, cold, frightened, excited, all at the same time. She wondered if this was the kind of mixed-up anticipation you felt before you died.

A figure emerged from the shadows at the end of the street. As it moved into the sphere of the first streetlight, Maria could see it was a man. He was tall, fair-skinned, and naked. He had long, blond hair that danced away from his head in messy dreads. His eyes were focused on Maria as he marched toward her.

Maria knew him. Not as the trickster who had somehow swapped her body and brought her to this place, or as the creature who had just transformed from newborn baby to man in a matter of minutes (though he was both of these, she somehow knew), but as the lover she'd had years before when she was in college.

It was a brief, passionate affair that ended Maria's virginity as well as her safe, staid existence. She had always been the good girl, the obedient daughter/sister/girlfriend. Now she was used and pregnant and desperate. Unwilling to face the dismay of friends and family or her former lover's recrimination, she had an abortion and moved away to rebuild a quiet life for herself.

The man smiled as he approached and suddenly the puzzle that was Maria's memory completed itself and expanded, until she understood things she should have never known. But that's how it worked, she thought with a waning wryness. The villain always revealed the full picture before dispatching his victim.

She had seen him that morning of her last day, but didn't register it at the time. Her life was a happy routine and things that fell outside of it she generally left outside of it. Instead, she went to rehearsal and performed that evening, where she encountered the poor woman who had died giving birth.

To him.

If Jesus was the product of a pure and virginal birth, it only made sense that God's former favorite would be born of darkness and death. When Jesus died and was reborn, he brought redemption and hope before ascending to his father's side. Each time this first fallen angel was reborn, he brought despair and misery. In his attempt to regain his place in the sun, he devoured his hosts' energy and eventually the bodies they gave birth to, forcing him to start the cycle again and again.

"You disappointed me once," he said, stroking her hair, and his touch reminded her of her college self, of his seduction and his assurances and her own shame, guilt, and flight.

"Your defiance proves your power." He smiled widely, a mockery of expression without warmth or true emotion. "Your strength will make me Legion."

"The Lord is my shepherd, I shall not want--"

He was upon her. Maria fell backwards into the grass by the curb. It was soft, cool, damp. His breath was hot and dry on her stomach as he loosened and removed her shorts.

She could feel.

She looked down, and realized she was back in her own body. She felt a moment of joy in finding something safely familiar, then let out a cry of horror.

She could *feel*. She was no longer in the cold, numb body of a dead woman. She was back where he could do her the most harm.

He lifted his head briefly to look at her, and there was no lust or desire on his face, only rage. This body was a vessel for a purpose--to be filled, drained, torn apart, and discarded while she suffered within it.

Maria knew at the moment he spread her legs and dropped his head between them that the pain would be endless. And she knew he would take pleasure in that. And she knew that logically, physically, he was not able to do what he was doing, but she could already feel his fingers probing and pulling him farther and farther into her womb.

With each inch of his body that disappeared into her, Maria let go of a bit of her sanity. Sometime after he was safely inside, sometime after he made her carry the burden of his diabolical being, she would birth him back into the world and his cycle would begin again. And he would live on, longer, stronger this time until his mortal shroud began to wear and he sought a new lover-mother.

And Maria realized, with his last few thrusts and the end of her fully conscious thought, there was nothing she could do about it this time.

Nameless

She has come here to die.

It has been only six weeks since one of her colleagues commented on how fatigued she looked. Five weeks since the first tests came back inconclusive. Three weeks since the diagnosis. One hour this afternoon to pack up her belongings, look around at the efficiency apartment she's called home for the past eleven years and wonder how long it will be before she is missed.

Metastasize. An awkward, ugly word she rolls around silently on her tongue. There is a hint of the spearmint gum she used to hide the taste of tears and vomit after she met with her doctor this morning. She tells no one this latest bad news, tells no one of her planned flight. There is no one to tell. And she realizes that worse than wondering how long it is before she's missed, is wondering how long it will take for her to be forgotten.

She climbs into her car and begins to drive. When she reaches the Chesapeake Bay Bridge she understands for the first time how some people are unable to make it across. The bridge span arcs upwards across the water. For long stretches you can't see the road ahead, and it looks as though you could drive off the edge and be suspended between sky and sea forever. She is already on the bridge, and now comes to the first of those ghostly stretches. She hesitates, her foot poised over the pedals. But for her, there is no choice. She heads toward a nowhere tiny town on Maryland's eastern shore, where her ancestors were brought to work as slaves on small plantations and never left. Now they are all dead.

And she has come to join them.

* * *

When she approaches the familiar house, she slows down, but tells herself she will not stop. The white paint is flaking, the green trim is faded, the yard is overrun with hardy weeds, thick-stemmed and prickly. The downstairs windows are cracked or broken, but the upstairs windows are intact and shadowed in the late afternoon autumn light. She looks at the upper window on the right, the one that was her room, and tries to remember if she was happy there. A dark face appears at the window and she slams on the brakes and parks the car in the middle of the dirt road.

The face seems to be moving, mouthing things to her. It is bloated, irregular, unfamiliar. She is cold, trembling, but forces herself to get out of the car. Perhaps there is someone like herself inside, needing comfort or companionship. She forces her way through the weeds and up the front steps. The front door is unlocked, and she enters.

Home was not the place of hugs from daddy and kisses from mommy. No games with siblings while snatching fresh-baked cookies from the counter of a large and airy kitchen. The first ten years of her life were spent here, in this tiny two-bedroom house - underfoot and under the thumb of her maternal grandmother. The other black children in the area were sent to live with relatives in big towns and cities to get their education, away from the clutches of the local troublemakers in the Klan. She and her grandmother had only each other. So she spent her afternoons (following morning lessons with her grandmother) carefully exploring the woods and backroads of the area, discovering magical places she kept to herself.

The downstairs is empty. She is afraid to call out, and afraid to go upstairs. She hears humming, and tries to remember if her grandmother ever sang to her. The humming is soft, consistent, and she imagines climbing the creaking stairs, opening the door to her old room, and approaching the back of an old rocker that held her baby doll when she was good and held her sore bottom when she was bad and had to sit facing the corner.

She can't make herself move. She's afraid of finding someone or something, and more afraid of finding nothing. She will not admit it, but more frightening than the face in the window or the prospect of dying is the dull realization that she really is all alone.

She looks around the empty space. There's the small hole in the wall for the sink plumbing, the scars in the paint for the cabinets and countertop where her grandmother cooked each meal on a hot plate. She closes her eyes and can almost smell the chicken frying in oil and the biscuits sizzling in butter. The soothing sound from above is no longer a lullaby, but a call to dinner. Her mouth is watering.

Meals were the only thing celebrated in this house. As a little girl she looked forward to each meal, not just because she spent most of the time in between each meal hungry, but because it was the one time she could see the light of living in her grandmother's face.

She opens her eyes, and remembers where she is and why she has come back. She walks over to a window facing the back of the property. Off to the left is the old county church, its clapboards still white and well tended. Beyond the church, behind a low wrought iron fence, is a small graveyard. But this is not where she has come to die.

The sun is sinking rapidly behind the trees and she feels the temperature dropping. She looks around the kitchen one more time before leaving. Outside, she pauses on the top step. She can no longer hear the humming. She walks to the car and looks back at the upstairs window. There is no face. Just a large mass of quivering bees and shifting shadows.

* * *

She works on automatic pilot now, afraid that her memory of the place she's trying to reach will fade with the evening light. The car stops running a few minutes later, just as she's turned left where the road ends in a "T." The gas gauge is on empty. She grabs her backpack of clothes and the tent and sleeping bag she picked up from a secondhand store on the way out of town. Her sacks of food and water seem heavy, though they're only enough for a week, longer even than the doctor has given her.

The road is narrow and would have been a jarring ride, but still easier than carrying her things up and over the ruts, tree roots, and gopher holes. After a half mile she wonders if she can go on, wonders if she is going the right way, if she has missed a turn through the trees, or if she should just drop her things in this lonely wooded place and give up. But after a few more steps she can see the clearing. It is much less open than when she was last here, nearly forty years ago.

In the years following her grandmother's death it was her memories of this place that kept her going while she was in the orphanage in Baltimore. She pretended the trees had grown close together to form the building's walls, and convinced herself the hard floors and small concrete play area merely kept the grass safe from the driving spring rain, the scorching summer sun, the howling autumn wind, and the biting winter snow. The other children didn't seem to mind. Maybe they didn't know any better. She tried to find out, tried to tell them what it was like out here in the country. At the time, she had little experience interacting with anyone other than her grandmother. She learned quickly that it is wisest to never open up to others; that way you never leave yourself open to harm.

She shakes off the memories and takes another look around. In front of her, the trees hold captive a large, dilapidated wooden shack in the middle of a meadow marked in regular patterns of fieldstone. She knows from her grandmother's stories that the shack served as a church in the 1800s; a place where the slaves could come and talk and sing and worship in secret.

She moves to the doorway and peeks inside. There are no pews or chairs. The walls bear some carvings, but none are from the people who have been cradled by the ground around here for two centuries. The graves are only hinted at by those broken pieces of fieldstone outside. Many of the markers have fallen over or been broken by vandals. None of the stones bear any inscriptions.

She leaves her bags near the front of the building, grabs a flashlight, and walks to the back, toward what's left of the pulpit area. As she picks her way through the dirt, weeds, and animal droppings covering the plank flooring, she scans for a place to clear debris and set up camp. She reaches a wooden altar that has been crushed by beams that appear to have only recently fallen in from the back portion of the roof. On the side of the altar facing her is a large hole, and she sweeps it with the flashlight to make sure there are no animals nesting inside. Instead, she sees what appears to be a box.

She struggles with it, her muscles weakened by her journey, her breathing weakened by her illness. When it pops free the force pushes her back onto her heels and then she falls forward again, kneeling. The box is made of woven reeds, perhaps from the cattails ringing the pond back in the other direction on the road. She opens it and gasps. Inside is a small book, made of stitched-together pages between plain bark covers. The handwriting is small and uneven, but she has no doubt this is a registry of the church members and the small drawing beside their names is a map of their burial plots in the surrounding field.

She rubs her finger carefully down the list of names, and finds a surname that matches her own. She knows firsthand that the exploration and documentation of slave graveyards is timely and difficult, and rarely rewarded with an artifact like the one she holds in her hands. Back in what she already thinks of as her "other life," a discovery like this would have made her year as an historian on local history.

She feels a strong urge to light a candle on the broken altar and give thanks for the gift. But the daylight is gone and she has more important things to tackle. She stands, finds her way back to her belongings, and clears a space near the front and off to the side, where the remaining roof cover seems to be the strongest. She has a peanut butter sandwich and some bottled water for dinner, and falls asleep dreaming of chicken and biscuits and fresh honey.

* * *

There is a sound in her head. It's low, like the buzzing bees, but there are words this time. She listens harder. She can't understand them, but she understands the emotion behind them. She opens her eyes.

The small church is filled with bodies. Or rather, the memory of bodies that once were. Skins once black are grey with death. She stares at the stiff backs of men, women, and children sitting on the floor. Some of the bare backs are marked with scars, raised and puckered like giant earthworms.

Her lips rear back at the sight, as if in their rapid flight they might pull open her jaws and allow the scream inside to escape. But a lifetime of stoicism prevails, and the sound is buried within, trapped in a brittle nest of unexpressed emotions.

Something scuttles past her legs and she flinches. The creature stops and turns to look at her. A little girl, so thin that she can't tell if the bumps on her back are scars or bones jutting through. The girl moves again, crawling quickly on all fours, keeping her face impossibly turned backwards as she melts into the crowded congregation.

She feels a ripple pass through them all, then realizes she's *seeing* it too, watching as their bodies distort like each one is passing through a curtain of water. And she knows now she must be dreaming because she's too calm and there are no such things as ghosts and she's not on any medication that could explain this away.

In unison, the men, women, and children turn their heads to stare at her. The whites of their eyes glow like thin wafers, swallowed by the darkness of their pupils.

She realizes she can still hear their voices, but their mouths are all closed.

* * *

In the morning, when she awakens, the book of names has moved from its spot near her pillow to the center of the floor where the figures sat last night. She has never been a sleepwalker, but then, she's never had dreams like that, either.

The air is cold, and the sky doesn't promise that the day will get warmer. She is too tired to hike through the woods, so instead she strolls around the meadow, counting the marker stones, counting the names in the book, counting the number of hours she may have left.

That night she warms a can of soup with a small camping torch, fearing perhaps the peanut butter led to the weird dream of the night before. Just in case, she stays awake reading a book, one of the few she brought with her. As the night wears on, her flashlight dips in unison with her head. She nods off, then jerks back awake several times. At one point the flashlight drops slowly from her hand and rolls down the slope of the uneven floor, thumping and bumping until it comes to a stop. She bounces her sleepy head upright and looks to where the flashlight has come to rest, casting its beam toward the back of the church. She glances nervously in that direction and almost cries with relief when she sees that the church is empty.

Without the glow of the light, the air around her suddenly feels cooler. She slides forward in her sleeping bag and leans out to grab the wayward flashlight. Her hand brushes something cold and hard beyond the light's handle. She watches shadowy digits rise and fall, unable to tell in the darkness if they are fingers or toes, tapping silently on the wooden floor. She pulls back quickly, away from the light, and shrouds herself in her sleeping bag. With her eyes squeezed tightly closed, she finds herself humming the tune from the night before.

The sun is high in the sky when she stretches out of her sleeping bag. Her back hurts from sleeping upright all night, hunched over her knees. Her arms are stiff, and she's annoyed to find she left the flashlight on all night and the batteries are dead.

Outside, the meadow is painted in frost the sun can't seem to melt. She stoops beside one of the larger markers, balancing her hand on its damp surface. The cold, unyielding stone reminds her of the unidentified limb from last night's dream.

* * *

It's almost evening when she gets the idea, and hurries into the church to dig through her backpack. The kitchen knife won't be strong enough, but the utility knife will probably work. She runs back outside and chooses one of the small stones, lifting it carefully from its spot and securing it on her lap as she consults the book of names and carefully begins to carve.

She works by torch and moonlight now. Her speed quickens as she becomes more familiar with the tool and the stone, but the cold begins to numb her fingers and has triggered a cough. She feels a spasm in her chest, the pain spreading to her back and down into her tailbone. She remembers refusing her doctor's offer for pain medication, feeling a need to punish herself for some sin she can't even remember.

Back inside the shack, she pulls off her cold clothes and pulls on layers of warm, dry, winter wear. Her eyes shine with excitement. She has scratched the rightful names onto six of the marker stones. The cuts are shallow, uneven, the handwriting shaky, but she has to sacrifice aesthetics to save the blade for the other twenty-one graves.

She coughs again, a familiar metallic taste coating the back of her throat. She warms some water and mixes in powdered hot chocolate. She almost feels content, and wonders if this is how it feels when her co-workers go camping with their families, or their children's scout troops. She wonders a lot these last couple of days about the things missing in her life. Not so much about the things themselves, but whether or not she *should* miss having close friends, a partner, a family, a place to call home.

At work, her co-workers talked about these things only to each other; around her, over her, as if she weren't sitting at the lunch table at all. She knows they thought she was haughty and distant when in fact; she remained silent because she had nothing of her own to share. She silently thanks her colleague for pointing out the early signs of her illness, though she knows it was done as a way to chip away at her icy shell, not to carefully thaw out the cold and lonely person underneath.

She puts down her mug. The voices fill her head again but the song is different, a little more hopeful. Suddenly, she is surrounded on all sides by sunken faces, closing in on her, trying to tell her something with their eyes. She knows now she's not dreaming. None of this has been a dream. She has fallen *in between*, like the souls surrounding her. There is no going back for her, but she craves and fears the companionship they offer following the lonely, uncertain journey that lies ahead.

The volume of the chorus increases, and she feels her heartbeat rise in a matching rhythm. Still, she will not cry out, will not cry, even when the gallery of eyes around her expand impossibly into darkness until all is black and she's left only with an impression of their presence in the feeble moonlight through the roof. She can't breathe, can't feel her extremities, but there is a warmth in the core of her body that makes her feel like this might be her time to go. As she waits for the end, she notices the grey forms are fading, and as they do, she realizes her aches and pains from the day fade with them.

* * *

The next day she carves ten names. She eats only a little breakfast, works through lunch, and stops in the evening only as her hand begins to shake and her vision blurs. She stumbles inside for a few sips of water and decides to lie down for a little while. At rest, she can feel the pain begin to well up behind her eyes, in her throat as she swallows, in her chest as she breathes, in her knees and ankles, in the hand that has been clenched tightly to knife and stone for nearly twelve hours.

She knows they're back, knows they've surrounded her again, but the song is even lovelier than before and she keeps her eyes closed so she doesn't spoil the hearing of it. Still, she can feel them hovering over her slack form, and she wonders if they are puzzled by her smile.

The singing fades. The pain fades. Her smile fades, as she begins to fully understand what it means.

She sleeps through most of the next day. Her head feels heavy and full of disconnected thoughts. Her arms and legs do not want to cooperate. Her jaw is slow to open and close, so she sips on water and soup, cold from the can.

When night comes, she waits for them. As she suspects, less than half remain. They sit stiffly, silently, facing forward. They do not sing. They do not look at her. They do not stay long.

* * *

The morning sky smells like rain, and she sets feverishly to work, knowing what the end will mean for both her and them. Shortly after noon the sky grows heavy with mist, then a steady drizzle that settles in as if it's always been. By the time she finishes the last scratch on the last headstone she is soaked and shivering. Her back hurts and her feet are numb, so she crawls through the mud and up into the shack where she collapses onto her damp bedding.

It is several hours before she can move again. She rolls over to her pack and dumps it out onto the floor. A short pillar candle falls onto the softened wood of the floor. She takes a deep breath, grips the candle and book of names tightly, pushes herself to her feet, and staggers to the altar. She places the book back in its box and back in the hole where she found it. She places the candle on top of the altar and lights it with the last gasps from the torch in her jacket pocket. Then she sinks to her knees and falls forward onto the floor, unconscious.

As before, the voices bring her to life. They sing a song of happiness and sadness, and she doesn't want it to end. She opens her eyes and cries at the beauty of the tiny points of light around her. Each candle matching her own, burning brightly in the air that has been washed clean and dried by the wind.

The bodies around her are no longer grey; she has brought *them* to life, if only briefly, in shades of brown and black, with flesh she can feel as they stop to touch her before stepping out into the night. Each hand warms her, but each person that leaves takes away a bit of the radiance until finally she is left alone, with only the echo of their touch and the halo of her own light.

She moves back to her spot, climbing inside her sleeping bag and singing softly to herself--a song to which she now knows the words. As she sleeps, her candle bends to one side, and just as stubbornly carves out its own space on the altar. As the flames move slowly across the shack, the smoke begins to rise, but hovers at the top of the trees before settling down like a mist, hiding the contents of the fiery meadow.

* * *

In the spring, a young man and an older woman arrive in a car and park in front of the clearing. The clover is flowering, spilling yellow over the tops of some of the stones arranged around the field. The man gets out of the car and looks questioningly over at the woman.

"This is it?"

"Yes," she says with a sigh. "This is the place, Kevin." She looks at him. "I've been here before, you know. My family owned a farm near here. For generations we had that farm. Used to own slaves, too, I'm sorry to say."

She coughs, deep and wet, her skinny sides ballooning in and out with each heave. Kevin looks away. It's not that long a drive from the university, but he is already weary of the sound of her suffering.

"There used to be a girl about my age who would come here to play. I'd follow her and watch her. She saw me one day, asked me to come play with her, to keep her company, but I couldn't. Wasn't allowed, you know--things were different back then between blacks and whites. I found out later we were actually related. Distant cousins."

Kevin glances back at the woman, this post-middle-aged relic of a time before he was born. He looks at her wrinkled face and blond hair gone mostly grey and wonders why what's-her-name is even here with him on this mapping project.

"Okay, let's get started," he says, moving out into the field.

The woman watches him for a minute. She is saddened by the way he dismisses her talk, her guilt, her need to relate. He walks around the site, stopping occasionally to look at the stones or push aside the vegetation covering some of the fallen markers. His fingers are large, brown, and strong. Her own are pale, frail, and tremble slightly as she pulls a notebook containing graphing paper out of a bag in the back of the car.

"There are probably fewer than thirty graves in here," the woman says, coming up behind him, "but they're only marked by these stones, and the university and the state don't want us disturbing them, just mapping them."

"What good is the map going to do?"

"It'll let the state know how many graves are out here and where they are. That way, if someone ever decides to put up some kind of development, they won't be disturbing a burial ground."

"What I mean is, all of these stones are blank. There's no way to know who's buried here."

The woman walks past him to a barren spot in the middle of the meadow. She closes her eyes. She remembers there used to be a shack here the slaves used as a church. That's where the little black girl used to spend most of her time when she came here to play.

"That old shack burned down years ago," the owner of the general store back in town had told her when she and Kevin stopped for gas. "Burned to the ground, and nothing's grown back in that spot since."

The woman opens her eyes and stoops to rub a hand over a couple of the stones near the site of the former church. Their surfaces are rough but unmarked. Kevin is right; none of the stones have any names on them.

She straightens suddenly. "Do you hear that?"

"Hear what?"

"Singing. Faint, but..."

"What kind of singing?"

"I don't know, I can't understand the words."

"Maybe it's from that church a few miles back."

"It's Friday. Besides, there's no wind. The sound wouldn't carry this far."

"Maybe it's bees. I saw some flying around. They probably have a hive nearby. Anyway, I don't wanna be out here forever," Kevin says, taking the notebook out of her hands and moving to the far left corner of the meadow to start marking the grave sites on the graph.

The woman moves to follow, stops, and turns back. The sunlight flares and she covers her eyes. She feels a chill. She lowers her hand and sees a faint outline of the ancient shack and a familiar figure in the doorway, beckoning to her. She takes a step, hesitates, and then stops, coughing once again.

"Are you coming?" Kevin turns and calls out to her.

She hears his voice, but the words are reflected on the lips of the figure in the ghostly church.

Are you coming?

Suddenly the church is full of bodies, their eyes all questioning her.

Are you coming?

She shakes her head.

"Not yet," she whispers to the crowd.

The figure in the doorway stops beckoning and smiles. It's all right.

They know she'll be joining them soon.

About the Author

Michelle Mellon discovered her love of writing at the age of nine. She was a published poet starting in high school and into her twenties, when she shifted her focus to short fiction.

In addition to the ever-bizarre world around us, Ms. Mellon draws inspiration from her experiences growing up as an Army dependent, and her varied occupations as dental assistant, project manager, copywriter, and communications manager.

In August 2015, she and her husband relocated from San Francisco to Germany, where Ms. Mellon has been a stay-at-home cat mom while finishing her story collection, writing for speculative fiction anthologies and magazines, and publishing a blog about her expat adventures.

She recently joined a software startup as a content writer and is close to completing her second fiction collection.

For updates on her work, visit her website www.mpmellon.com and/or follow her on Twitter: @mpmellon

Other HellBound Books Titles Available at: www.hellboundbookspublishing.com

Them

Ray Sanders returns home from Florida to bury his mother.

Soon, the supernatural evidence behind his mother's demise begins to surface in the form of dreams and mysterious happenings.

During all of the madness, Sanders must face his destiny and vanquish the generations-old evil that has plagued his family since the 1800's…

In 1854, Louis Sanders, with the help of Elias Atkins, dug a well to provide water to the family farm. What they did not anticipate was the water to be infested with Odomulites - ancient sins. These malevolent beings - were trapped in our world on their way to the spirit world - formed a pact of protection with both Sanders and Atkins; the families would serve as guardians of the Odomulite nests and in return, a blind eye would be cast when the Odomulites took host bodies to inhabit and feed upon. It was this pact, which in 2016 would propel Sanders and Julie Fontaine - a young woman with a special connection to the Spirit World - into the heart of the last active nest to rid the town of its insidious Odomulite population.

Blood in The Woods

Based upon true events...For Jody, growing up in the late eighties and early nineties in the small Louisiana town of Hammond with his best friend Jack was filled with wonderful childhood memories.

Time is spent playing in the woods, shooting pellet guns, enjoying blowing up mailboxes, fighting at school and upon the dawning of interest in the fairer sex, their carefree lives typical of children with few responsibilities and no worries beyond the next pop-quiz or getting to second base. As they grow older together and experience the joys and pains of life, love, family and friendship, they uncover a grim secret that their home town has kept, and through little more than an innocent, idle curiosity, Jody and Jack stumble upon something horrific in the woods and their lives quickly take a most sinister and dangerous turn as they find themselves hunted by an unspeakable evil...

War Game

The tenants never saw it coming.

The Murray building, constructed in the seventies by the eccentric billionaire Samuel Murray, contains a secret so horrific and abhorrent that those caught up in his nefarious social experiment might never see the light of day again.

Time is ticking.

Only one person can beat the War Game and walk away with a cool $100 million in cash.

Who dies? Who lives? Who is the real villain? What is the building's biggest secret, and why do only a select few know about it?

War Game is a brutal, maniacal thriller with enough plot twists to make your head spin and your stomach churn. There's violence aplenty, murder, mayhem, and buckets of blood…

Can you predict the outcome?

Dead is Dead; But Not Always

A wonderfully eclectic collection of disturbingly good short stories…

The mountain winds howl and blood flows to appease, tradition runs deep and transforms the skin for the sake of togetherness.

Buried beneath the soil is a book to bridge the eternal dark with the light of life.

God's way is with a hiss but Satan's way is with a kiss, and in the Arctic only the bears can hear your screams.

When it's your time go the lake will tell you, and being a kid ain't easy when the natural and supernatural collide to peel the layers from your back.

From dread to thriller to cosmic, the seven novelettes collected here meld into one bone-jarringly bleak outing, bound to rattle cores and test readers' nerves.

Dead is Dead, but Not Always is the first solo collection from Canadian author Eddie Generous.

Demons, Devils and Denizens of Hell: Vol, 2

The second volume in HellBound Books' outstanding horror anthology fair teems with tales of Hades' finest citizens – both resident and vacationing in our earthly realm… -

Compiled by the inimitable P. Mattern and featuring: Savannah Morgan, Andrew MacKay, Jaap Boekestein, James H Longmore, Stephanie Kelley, Ryan Woods, James Nichols, P. Mattern, Marcus Mattern, Gerri R Gray, and legion more…

Shopping List 2: Another Horror Anthology

Once again, HellBound Books brings you an outstanding collection of horror, dark, slippery things, and supernatural terror - all from the very best up and coming minds in the genre.

We have given each and every one of our authors the opportunity to have their shopping lists read by you, the most wonderful reading public, and have the darkest corners of their creative psyche laid bare for all to see...

In all, 21 stories to chill the soul, tingle the spine and keep you awake in the cold, murky hours of the night from: Erin Lee, The Truth Artist, John Barackman, Serena Daniels, M.R. Wallace, Isobel Blackthorn, Alex Laybourne, Jason J. Nugent, Josh Darling, Jovan Jones, Nick Swain, Douglas Ford, Craig Bullock, Craig Bullock, Jeff C. Stevenson, PC3, David F Gray, Sergio Palumbo, Donna Maria McCarthy, David Clark & Megan E. Morales

**A HellBound Books LLC
Publication**

http://www.hellboundbookspublishing.com

Printed in the United States of America